BY THE STANDING STONE

BY THE STANDING STONE

MAXINE TROTTIER

Stoddart Kids
TORONTO · NEW YORK

Published in Canada in 2000 by
Stoddart Kids,
a division of Stoddart Publishing Co. Ltd.
34 Lesmill Road
Toronto, Canada M3B 2T6
Tel (416) 445-3333 Fax (416) 445-5967
E-mail cservice@genpub.com

Published in the United States in 2001 by
Stoddart Kids,
a division of Stoddart Publishing Co. Ltd.
180 Varick Street, 9th Floor
New York, New York 10014
Toll free 1-800-805-1083
E-mail gdsinc@genpub.com

Distributed in Canada by
General Distribution Services
325 Humber College Blvd.
Toronto, Canada M9W 7C3
Tel (416) 213-1919 Fax (416) 213-1917
E-mail cservice@genpub.com

Distributed in the United States by
General Distribution Services, PMB 128
4500 Witmer Industrial Estates
Niagara Falls, New York 14305-1386
Toll free 1-800-805-1083
E-mail gdsinc@genpub.com

04 03 02 01 00 1 2 3 4 5

Canadian Cataloguing in Publication Data

Trottier, Maxine

By the standing stone

ISBN 0-7737-6138-1

I. Title.

PS8589.R685B9 2000 jC813'.54 C00-9310940
PZ7.T76By 2000

Cover and text design: Tannice Goddard
Cover illustration: Al van Mil

We acknowledge for their financial support of our publishing program the Government of Canada through the Book Publishing Industry Development Program (BPIDP), the Canada Council, and the Ontario Arts Council.

Printed and bound in Canada

For Bill, with all my love.

Fort Detroit
Alikisibi
Lake Erie
Lake Ontario
Oswego
Fort Niagara
The Oneida Castle
Albany
N
W
E
S
Boston
The Route From
Boston to Detroit
1773
by the hand of
Lord John MacNeil

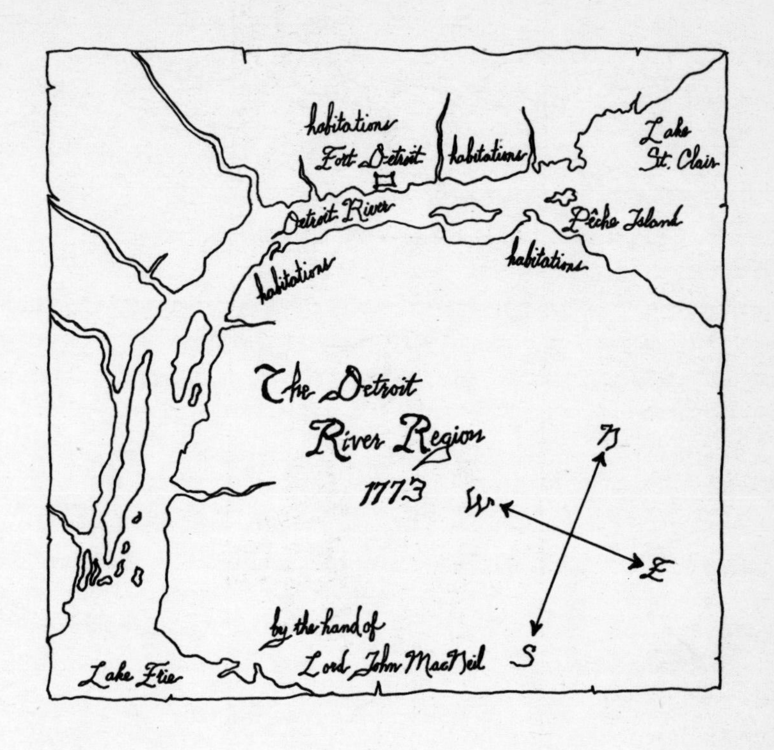
habitations
Fort Detroit
habitations
Lake
St. Clair
Detroit River
Pêche Island
habitations
habitations
The Detroit
River Region
1773
N
W
E
S
by the hand of
Lord John MacNeil
Lake Erie

Charlotte MacNeil was a true sailor. When fate set her on a new course, she left England and came to a land more exciting than any she could have imagined. But unfamiliar waters are dangerous for those upon them, and this was especially true in 1773. On a fine November morning, Charlotte would learn that all the sailors' knowledge in the world can be useless if you are suddenly swept away. Courage and instinct are all you have to steer by then. But that would come later. For now, there was only the thrill of wind and water and the new land that lay before her.

CHAPTER ONE

As he stood on the deck of *HMS Rampant* watching a small sailboat scud across the water, Jamie MacNeil shaded his eyes and peered into the sunlight that glittered over Lake Ontario. He could see that Mack was about to get a good drenching once again.

He did not need to be in the boat to know exactly how Mack's body would move with the vessel, balancing it against the force of the wind. They had sailed so often together. In fact, they had grown up in boats. Mack was a sailor through and through.

The wind blew in a steady gust from the mouth of the Niagara River. It shifted just enough to let Mack pull in the sail and drive the boat toward *Rampant*. Jamie could almost feel the trembling of the tiller in his own hand. There. Lean to starboard a bit and level her out. Haul in the sail, not too much now, and brace your feet against the hull. The wind will always pose a challenge, and your vessel must have the answer. How often had Mack said that to him?

"You are being soaked!" he called out cheerily through

cupped hands. He laughed as spray showered over Mack.

"It means nothing to me," the answer came back, and in a moment the boat was near the ship's side. Mack pulled hard on the tiller, bringing the bow sharply into the wind, and let the sheet run free. The sail flapped helplessly as the boat slowed. Jamie reached out for the length of line Mack tossed to him, then he tied the vessel securely to the ship's rail.

"Mack, you fool, you are dripping everywhere!" Jamie laughed again. He stepped back and pushed his hair from his eyes. "Where is your sense of dignity?"

Charlotte MacNeil looked up at him and smiled widely. Then she pulled herself onto the ship, struggling with her damp skirts.

"It is impossible to have one in this condition," she grumbled. Clear blue eyes looked levelly at Jamie and he stared back, his face straight. "It is why I prefer a man's clothes for sailing, as you well know. They may become just as wet, but at least I can move about in them."

"And where is your straw bonnet for the sun so that your nose does not freckle? You forgot your bonnet, Miss Charlotte MacNeil." They both laughed at his joke.

Mack wrinkled her sunburned, freckled nose at him. Then she turned her attention back to the boat, checking the line to make certain it would not slip. "Charlotte MacNeil's nose is beyond hope, I fear. But it does suit someone named Mack well enough."

"I think it is a grand nose," Jamie teased. "However, I do believe it has had enough sun for the day. See here —

I am off below. A book awaits my attention, I think. Will you join me, Mack?"

"Not just yet. I shall come down when I stop dripping," said Mack. She watched Jamie cross the deck and disappear down the companionway.

Alone, Mack stood at *Rampant*'s rail and watched wavelets shiver across the water. It was a mild day for mid-November, and the unusually warm wind that blew from the shore carried the scent of wood smoke from the buildings there. In the distance, Fort Niagara, with its imposing stone building, stood watchful against the blue sky. The British flag blew out stiffly. Mack imagined she could hear it snapping in the wind.

How odd to have heard her full Christian name come from her cousin's lips just now. No one had called her Charlotte in a very long while, not for the three years, in fact, since she had come to Canada with Jamie in 1770. He had begun calling her Mack during the long sea voyage.

"Mack?" wondered her guardian, Lord John MacNeil, the first day he had set eyes on her in Boston. "What happened to Charlotte?"

"I think Charlotte fell overboard," explained Jamie, keeping his face serious. "We are sailors now, John, and she needed a sailor's name."

"It suits you," John answered thoughtfully. "I decree it shall be your new name. You will have a new life with me here, and you might as well have a new name to go with it!" To everyone here she became Miss Mack.

How her life had changed since then. She was barely ten years old when she went to live at Brierly, John's family estate in England. Her parents had died of smallpox, as had John's father and brother David. John became Charlotte's guardian and, as such, they thought he would return home. Instead, John sent for her and his younger brother. Returning to Brierly held no more appeal to the new young Lord MacNeil then, than it did for Mack now. She and Jamie had been so happy with John. Now that might end.

I will turn back into Charlotte again, she thought as she walked the deck, and I am not certain at all that I am Charlotte anymore. Someone named Charlotte should be small and delicate, a young English lady with a pale complexion and unspoiled hands.

Mack had long legs, which were hard with the muscle that came from a summer on the lake, braced against the endless shifting of a moving ship. Then there was the slightly tanned, and thus unfashionable, skin and the hopelessly freckled nose.

No, I am more a Mack now than a Charlotte, she thought as the wind pulled at her heavy, damp skirts. Turning her back on Fort Niagara, she followed Jamie below.

Stopping at the door of the cabin in which John had his quarters, Mack opened it and walked in without knocking. She and Jamie were welcome there at any time, she knew. It was such a warm and curious room, filled with the odds and ends of things they had collected this summer. On the desk lay a quill made from the feather of a wild goose and the journal in which John often wrote. Books filled the shelves. The room smelled of beeswax and oiled leather. John's drawings lay in rolls and piles everywhere.

Jamie lay stretched out on the berth with a book in his hands. At thirteen he was only two years younger than she, yet Mack was taller and heavier by a good bit. Jamie was as slight and fine-boned as John had been at that age, and, with his straight dark hair and gray eyes, he did look a good deal like his brother. Jamie glanced up at her, smiled absently, and put his nose back into the book.

"You are still thinking of the letter," Jamie said from the depths of the volume. "Even sailing and a soaking did not knock it out of your head."

"I am not thinking of it at all," she answered sweetly, although she could see the cursed thing among the papers on John's desk. Jamie had read it aloud last night and Mack had almost been able to hear Jane's voice.

"My Dears," Jane had written. "We all trust you are well. It will be forever until you receive this letter. Our *Odonata* is a speedy vessel, but even it cannot cross the Atlantic any more quickly than the ocean and winds will allow. That I remember well from when, as a child, I wrote to John in Canada. How hard it was to be separated from him. As twins, we were very close to each other; I treasured each letter. It always seemed such a long time before I would have word back from him.

"I do hope *Odonata* will bring you all home to us soon. Mama, Henry and the children send their love. I, of course, do as well. I suspect John is letting the pair of you run absolutely wild, as he did himself when he was a boy. How splendid!

"Is Canada as wonderful as John has always said it is? What stories you will have to share when you come home once more. For Brierly is your home, Charlotte, as it is Jamie's. I know that when you return and are settled here with us, you will come to love it as much as I always have."

Jamie had continued to read aloud the happy news of the children and Jane's husband, Henry. Brierly was as beautiful as ever. But Mack barely heard Jamie's voice. Only the words of how they might have to return to England had rung in her mind.

Mack shook herself slightly, as if to shake the memory of the letter from her thoughts. Jamie looked out from behind his book and watched her thoughtfully. If he had not known her so well, he would have considered her a cold person indeed. She seemed indifferent and distant, but she was not. The young men who met her soon lost interest, for she held them all at arm's length with her clipped speech and uptilted nose. Jamie knew her other side, the warmth and good humor, and they were the closest of friends.

"You are not only thinking of the letter, you are planning something against it. I know you. This has been a wonderful time, Mack, has it not?" said Jamie. "I would no sooner go back than you. I have not once had to wear a wig!"

Mack loved him dearly. Had they not shared so much as children, playing in the gardens at Brierly, chasing each other through the orchard of young apple trees? But Jamie's life there would not be hers.

"Yes, well, returning to England for you may mean little more than having to once again wear a wig, Jamie. It means other things for me. When I return to England, it will be to marry," she said emptily, as she looked out the windows at the back of the cabin. "Oh, not at once, of course, but it will happen as surely as you lie there before me. I am nothing more than a chattel."

"That is the most utter nonsense!" Jamie sputtered, slamming shut the book. "Who would marry you? Have you someone in mind? Of course, you do not. And you are not a chattel at all. What *is* a chattel?"

Mack turned to him, bright spots of red on her cheeks and neck. "Property. You see, that "utter nonsense" is the law. If my father had lived, I would be his property. That doubtful privilege is John's now, since I am his ward. If I wed, I belong to my husband, and if I bear children and am widowed, I am the property of my son. This hardly presents a happy thought, given the way we have lived here."

They had enjoyed a quiet freedom with John. Oh, his house of squared log timbers on Pêche Island was far removed from the grandeur of the huge, old building that was Brierly. Still, it had become home to her. There, she did not feel a guest. She did not feel she had been taken in out of pity, as she often had at Brierly. With John, she felt treasured and safe, just as she knew Jamie did.

They had wandered the island's beaches and explored the Detroit River and parts of Lake Erie with John. He had a boat that he kept moored in a cove on the island, a sloop of fifty feet called the *Swift*. It had once belonged to the Scot, Wallace Doig. John had sailed on it with him and the Seneca, Natka, as a boy. Since Wallace no longer sailed out so much himself, he had given the *Swift* to John. Carefully maintained for these years, it was still a fine old vessel. What a pleasure it was to anchor in some quiet inlet and listen to John's stories of his boyhood. Then, to sleep under the stars, bundled in a feather quilt with not a care, was wonderful.

"Ridiculous. No one will ever make you his property or force you to marry. John would not allow it! I will not allow it!" Jamie said stoutly. "Never fear, Mack, I will take care of you."

Mack rolled her eyes at Jamie and poked him in the ribs. He doubled in laughter and squirmed away from her. Likely, it would be the other way around. Jamie's health had improved in the years since they had left England, his color was much better and he no longer coughed constantly, but she always felt she must watch over him.

She looked down at the book he had been reading. *Robinson Crusoe*. It was a tale of great adventure and sailing and pirates. Well, she had an idea for an outing this afternoon that would offer them some adventure. Perhaps it would wipe the idea of leaving from both their thoughts.

"Let us just say we will take care of each other," she said dryly. "We shall both need all the help we can get if we must go back to England. Can you imagine the stuffiness of it after Canada and the colonies? I, for one, prefer not to. But enough of this, Jamie." She turned from him and began to root around in a trunk, pulling out first one, and then another, piece of clothing. “Yes. These will do quite nicely.”

“Oh, no, Mack!” said Jamie as he sat up and let his book drop to the bedding. “I know very well what you are planning. And you are taking John’s breeches and shirt and stockings again without asking! What would he say?”

Mack turned to him and smiled widely. “He would tell you to turn your back while I change!” Jamie snorted and flipped over.

“I do not have a good feeling about this,” he grumbled into the pillow.

“And since you ask, I expect John would say that his clothing fits me very well, just as he always does,” Mack went on cheerfully. Out of her bodice, shift, and petticoat, she quickly pulled on John’s stockings, breeches, and shirt. “What would you have me do, Jamie? You know I cannot sail comfortably in a bodice and skirts. You may turn around now. I am quite decent.” She looked innocently at Jamie and he glared back, his face serious.

“That is just the point. John does not like you sailing out on your own. And you will go ashore. I can read you like this book! When John is here it is quite another matter, but it is not safe for you to leave the ship alone with soldiers everywhere,” Jamie warned.

“I will not be alone at all. You will be with me!” She grinned at the expression of horror on his face, but she knew he would follow her anywhere.

"If he sees us, Mack, it will be bread and water for a week," Jamie muttered to himself, although he knew perfectly well John would do no such thing. He gave up. It was hopeless to argue with her. For Mack, the sheer joy of the moment was well worth any scolding that might follow.

"He will not see us, and if he does, he will surely understand how important it is to have a sail on such a fine day. The good weather cannot last much longer. Come, now." She pulled on one of John's coats and she was ready. There was only her pouch to tie at her waist and moccasins to fetch from their cabins.

They hurried down the companionway and out onto the deck. A few of the ship's crew were there, but none of the common sailors would have said a word to stop the relatives of Lord MacNeil. Patterns of cats' paws danced here and there where the breeze touched the lake. First Mack, then Jamie, climbed down into the sailboat. Mack untied the line and, giving a hard push against the ship's hull, set the sailing vessel free. Jamie pulled hard on the halyard to raise the single canvas sail. When it began to fill with wind, Mack hauled on the sheet, drew in the sail, and steered away from the ship.

The boat cut speedily through small, foam-specked waves. Jamie took the sheet from her, pulled hard on it to trim the sail further, and the boat heeled over as it began to pick up speed. Mack could feel the trembling of the tiller in her hand. They both leaned to starboard a bit and the hull became level.

Mack's hair streamed out in the wind; her ribbon

floated in the wake far behind them. The hull hissed across the water and spray sparkled everywhere. Mack's breeches and loose shirt became splashed and damp, as did Jamie's clothing. Droplets wet their faces. Jamie laughed out loud at the sight of Mack dripping once again, then turned his head and looked toward the beach. They did seem to be approaching it rather quickly.

"We will crash into the shore!" he called happily, as he glanced back at her.

"Not a chance! I am a better sailor than that!" Mack shouted back, and in a moment the boat was but a dozen wave lengths from the beach.

Mack gave the tiller a hard pull to bring the bow into the wind. Jamie let the sheet run out through his hands, air spilled from the sail, and the boat slowed. Jamie jumped awkwardly into the lake and grabbed for the thwarts. Mack leaped out at the same moment, and together they guided the boat to the beach. Laughing and gasping with the cold water, they dragged the sailboat onto the pebbles. Mack tied a length of line to a huge driftwood log. Hand in hand they walked up the beach, the wet leather of their moccasins squishing with each step.

Jamie dropped down to the coarse grass above the sand. Mack did the same. How fine the warm sun felt on her damp stockings and breeches. They leaned back on their elbows and watched the ship floating offshore in deep water. Even from here they could see the way *Rampant* strained at her anchor as the wind blew across the hull and through her rigging. She looked solid and solitary without the sailboat bobbing behind her.

Mack sat up and ran her hands through her thick hair, combing out the tangles with her fingers. Then she fished about in her pouch. Surely there was a ribbon there with all the other odds and ends? She pulled one out and tied back her hair. The dark tresses reached only to her shoulders. How horrified John had been when Jamie had chopped it off for her, but at this length it was much better for sailing and swimming. Mack stood and brushed off the seat of her breeches.

"Lovely," commented Jamie, following her. "Most elegant." She ignored his teasing, for she did not care how she appeared to anyone. If the clubbed hair and breeches made her look like a tall young boy, what did it matter?

"Let us walk," she suddenly suggested to Jamie. "We will dry quickly. It is a beautiful day, the sun is shining, and we have the beach to ourselves."

"Where will we go?" he asked. The wind was slowly dropping and a lone cricket sang in the quiet air as small waves hissed into the sand. A faint dusty scent of late wildflowers and crushed leaves drifted to Mack's nose. She would always remember it.

"Oh, I do not know," she answered carelessly, as she looked down the beach and then toward the mouth of the river. "Let us just walk and see where we end." And they took the first steps on a journey that would change their lives forever.

CHAPTER TWO

Jamie and Mack wandered down the beach toward the mouth of the river. Fort Niagara rose above them, but Mack knew that they could not be seen by John or anyone unless that person was practically hanging from the windows on the upper floor. They were sheltered from the wind and hidden in the lee of the cliff. Out on the lake gulls mewed like hungry cats, diving and squabbling for fish.

The sailing and the fresh air helped to clear her head. She looked up and thought of John and the words they had exchanged that morning. The scene was fresh in her mind.

"You are certain you will not come ashore with me?" he had asked her on the deck of *Rampant*.

"Absolutely certain. I will stay on board and find something to do below to keep busy."

"You are not still cross, are you?" John said a bit cautiously.

Mack knew he was referring to Jane's letter. "I am not cross at all," she answered. Only miserable, she thought.

She looked John over. His long dark hair was tied back. In heavy leggings and hunting coat, he was dressed for the journey he would make out into the land that lay beyond Fort Niagara. He carried a musket. A hunting bag, powder horn, and a worn document case were slung over his shoulders.

"It would be a change from the ship. We have lived aboard for months now," coaxed John. "Samuel is already waiting at the fort. Besides, there will be a friend I would have you meet."

"I require no changes at all, and I shall meet your friend when you all return," she said firmly, fixing her gaze upon him. "I have visited the fort many times since we have sailed here on Lake Ontario. You will enjoy yourself far more with Lieutenant Smith if I am not hovering in the background, impatient to return to the ship. Besides, I am in no state for proper company."

John smiled hopelessly, shaking his head at his ward. "You have salt water for blood, my girl. I know you would rather be here than on shore. And it is Lieutenant Colonel Francis Smith, if you please. He does hold fast to formalities."

Mack walked with John to the rail of the ship. He turned suddenly and, putting his arm around her, gave her a quick hug.

"Put the letter from your mind, Mack," he said. His voice was tender and filled with the affection he felt for her. "We will winter here at Niagara on the ship, if it pleases you, rather than at the fort. In time, you both shall return to England, at least for a while. You have always known that. But it need not be for many months yet, perhaps not until next year, and it need not be forever. And I will go with you, Mack."

"Can we not simply return to the island until we have to go back to England?" Mack pleaded. "Wallace and Natka will be wondering what has become of us. They must be worried." The two old men had remained on the island at the house they had helped John build. They would spend the winter there as they always did.

John smiled. "Since they taught me all I know of the wilderness, I think they have faith that I can protect myself and you. I will send word yet again, though, that we will remain here for now."

"I have no desire to return to England at all, John," she said bleakly. "There is nothing for me there. My parents have been dead for years. I cannot even recall my own mother's face. It is not as though I am not fond of Jane and her family. I am, but Brierly has not ever truly been my home."

John sighed. "They wish to see you again, Mack," he said gently. "And do not forget Jamie. They are his family, as well."

She could not bear the way he was looking at her, and so she smiled as though none of this mattered.

"Consider it gone from my mind," she announced bravely. But it was not.

"Samuel and I shall return in two days, then. I will have a great many drawings to show you," John went on. "You will be safe here aboard the ship."

"I look forward to seeing your drawings. Fare thee

well, John," she said as he kissed her forehead.

John had climbed down carefully into the canoe. He settled his weapon and gear, then picked up a paddle. Casting off the line that tied the canoe to the ship, Mack tossed it to him and watched John paddle away. He turned once to wave. Later she would remember his warm smile and wish that she had returned it.

Continuing along the beach, Mack sighed as her mind returned to the present. She had been paying little heed to Jamie walking on ahead. Mack stopped now and again, searching the sand at the line where the highest of the waves reached. There she found the best treasures. She kept a glass bottle in her cabin, into which she dropped the tiny objects, small bones, or pebbles, memories of days on one lake or another.

Mack stopped and crouched. Her finger poked at something half hidden in the damp sand. She set the object in her palm and blew the grains away. It was a small fragment of bone, a pale medallion the size of a fingernail. She had more than a dozen like it in her pouch. She loosened the drawstring on the leather bag and dropped it in. John had told her that they were sheepshead stones.

"Sheepshead are common fish in the lakes and good enough eating. The stones come from the fish's skull," he said, rattling them in the palm of his hand. "Save them, Mack. They say the stones bring luck."

John knew everything about this land, Mack often thought. He did not seem precisely British to her. Nor was he like the Canadians, or even the Natives with whom he spent so much time. He was like some new creature honed by a wilderness that had worked its savage magic upon a young boy long ago. Sometimes he seemed aloof and distant, carefully edging his way through life, letting few people come too close. She could not know how much like him she was becoming.

Mack looked up and watched Jamie, who was now far ahead and walking briskly down the deserted beach. She would have called to him to come back, to walk with her, except that she did not wish to draw attention to themselves. The sound might carry up to the fort. She would have to run to catch him, and she felt too lazy to do that.

But then he turned. For a moment Jamie smiled warmly, and then his expression changed as his eyes shifted to the hillside. He began to run back. Mack looked over her shoulder. Six armed men were there. Two were already on the beach and the others were only feet away, skittering down through the grass. Jamie slid to a stop at her side in the loose sand.

"Say nothing," she warned in a whisper, gripping his arm. "I do not like the look of these men. Do not tell them who we are." She felt her skin creep as the men walked toward them.

"Why ever not?" Jamie whispered back, but Mack did not answer. She only held onto Jamie's arm, squeezing it so that he might mind her words.

The men were dressed in rough cloth shirts and leather leggings and moccasins. Their tunics were worn and dirty. Some of their clothing was stained in spots with what might have been old blood. They wore kerchiefs knotted over their greasy hair, and a rank odor came from them all, a foul combination of wood smoke and bodies that had not been washed in months. All of the men stopped and leaned casually against the muskets they propped in the sand. One of them walked slowly around Jamie and Mack, looking them up and down.

"Now what have we here, I ask myself?" he said. His accent was harsh and his voice whiskey-roughened. He rubbed a hand across the stubble on his cheek and, cupping his palm under his chin, tapped a finger against his jaw.

"I think it would be two fine lads out for a stroll on a fair afternoon, Ben," called one of the others.

Ben chuckled at this, for one of the "lads" was clearly a female. "Have you no eyes in your head, you fool? That is no boy!"

"Taking the air, don't you know?" said another and he minced around his musket. The men chuckled. To Mack there was no humor in the sound, only menace.

"Is it so?" asked the man they called Ben. "Are you taking a walk, my chicks?" He pushed his unshaven face close to Mack. She leaned away from the awful smell of rotten teeth and onions.

Ben Sparks was a heartless man. Like the others, he was a trapper and trader, but when opportunity arose he sold other things. Now and again he came upon a child alone, looking for berries or fetching water from the river, out of sight of family or homestead. Many young ones had disappeared to be sold as slaves or indentured workers by Sparks. For those who might care, Sparks faked papers of ownership. Seven years was not so very long for a girl to work as an indentured servant on an isolated farm. And the army was always open to the possibility of a strong young boy. Failing that, the Natives would buy children to replace those they lost to sickness or war. There was always a market somewhere.

"Leave us be," said Jamie in a brave voice. "We want no trouble from you." He shrugged his arm from Mack's grasp and, pushing her ahead of him, began to walk past the group.

"Not so quickly, lad," said Sparks in a hurt tone. Then the hand of one of the men flashed out and grabbed Jamie's wrist. "You cannot wander off just when we are all getting to know each other. Where's the manners your mama showed you?" The men nearly collapsed in laughter at this remark, but Mack felt rage boil up inside herself.

"Let him go!" she shouted as she swung at Ben's face. He easily dodged her hand and grabbed hold of it. The other man twisted Jamie's arm behind him and forced the boy to his knees on the beach. Jamie cried out in pain and anger.

"It seems these young ones need a bit of taming. Come along now," ordered Ben, and he twisted Mack's arm up behind her shoulder blades. She felt his breath harsh and rank against her cheek. He chuckled.

"Leave us alone!" she cried. She could not bear the sight of Jamie being hurt. From the anger on his face, he felt the same thing as he watched her.

"Hush now, my girl," laughed Sparks, and then he

whispered to Mack. "What a fine surprise you are." He looked up at Jamie. "It's a good price you will both bring. I could sell you to the Natives, my boy, but I think we may do a bit better elsewhere. And you, my chick, I think I may keep for myself." He twisted Mack's arm just a little harder. She fought to keep from groaning. "The sale of the boy will make us a good enough profit. The ropes, you dolts," he called to his comrades, and then he spoke in a sweetly poisonous voice to Mack. "If you struggle, I'll break your arm. And if you run, well, I think I will shoot you or poke you with my knife. Then your friend as well, since it will have put me in such a foul mood."

Mack tried to kick him, but he simply pulled harder and she dropped to the ground, gasping. She was strong, but she would never have been able to break loose from his powerful hands.

"I want no part of this, Sparks," said one of the men. He glanced nervously up at the stone building.

"Nor I," said another firmly.

"They are from the fort, of that I am certain, and there will be trouble over this, Sparks," said a third. "I'm away, and if you have any sense at all, you will release them."

"Your lips are sealed on this, if you are wise," Ben warned. "I trust you will give the fort a wide berth."

"It's your affair now," one of them answered, then they turned and headed off.

"You are fools," Ben Sparks murmured behind their backs as they walked away. Then he turned to the remaining men. "Are you two with me?"

"We are," they answered one after the other.

"Do not bother to think of yelling for help," said one of the remaining men as Jamie and Mack were pulled roughly to their feet. "Yelling for help always puts Ben in a foul mood. He does have his moods, does Ben." The men slipped coarsely braided thongs over Mack's and Jamie's necks. They tightened the nooses.

"Your names. What are they? And do not lie to me. I will know it at once," Sparks warned.

"He can smell a lie, Ben can," one of the men cackled.

Mack pressed her lips shut, defiance blazing in her eyes. But then Sparks pulled her very close to him. She shut her eyes. "I am Charlotte MacNeil. Mack, they call me. And he is Jamie MacNeil."

"Mack — what sort of name is that?" hooted one of Ben's followers.

"It is a fine name for this young chick," Ben Sparks shot over his shoulder, and the man stopped laughing at once.

"Yes. Very fine," he said in a small voice.

"Where are you taking us?" Jamie demanded, as the party started out. There was no choice but to follow; it was that or choke.

"You are a curious boy," answered Sparks, jerking on the thong just a bit. "But I do admire curiosity in the young, so I will give you a hint. Then you had best shut your mouth and keep it shut. I feel a mood coming on. Have you ever thought of how you would look in a red coat, lad?" Mack's belly clenched in fear as she stumbled along behind Sparks. The socket of her arm ached dully.

"A red coat? Whatever do you mean?" asked Jamie in an unbelieving voice. "What are you going to do to us?" Ben slapped his thigh and he laughed cruelly.

"Not the both of you, just yourself. The red coat? I wager you'll look grand in it, though it will not matter whether you do or not. You see, my lad, you're marching off to join King George's army!"

◇ ◇

Within the commandant's quarters, high above the beach, John rose from the chair across from Lieutenant Colonel Smith. John MacNeil was man of six and twenty years with appealing looks that the wilderness had chiselled. He had inherited his title after smallpox had killed his father and then his brother. Although English by birth, he had passed nearly half his life here in Canada and the colonies, traveling the land with one friend or another, drawing and painting the frontier for the Crown in England. King George had a great curiosity about his possessions; John's sketches had shown him the world that lay beyond the ocean. The King's gratitude had taken many forms. The use of the British warship was one. They had lived aboard *Rampant* since they had arrived from Pêche Island last spring on this sketching expedition.

The officer watched as John picked up his musket and prepared to take his leave after their visit. MacNeil was most pleasant company and a refreshing change from what passed for British culture in this place.

"There will be war, Lord MacNeil, and, mark my words, it will be long and hard. These colonials have no sense of loyalty to anything but themselves. It has always been so here and in Canada. They will turn on England like a pack of hungry dogs, for there is talk of revolution everywhere. We shall need such loyalists as yourself when the first shot is fired. And we will put it down — mark my words," Smith said firmly. "This land will be England's forever. To the health of King George, sir!" Raising his glass to his monarch in a toast, the officer smiled at John over the goblet of wine.

"To King George," echoed John as he drained his own glass. He had always been loyal to the Crown in his own way, drawing for the King, acting almost like a pair of eyes for the monarch. He no longer felt the same passion for it that he once had. Too many friends had been lost in wars and plagues. Too many years had been spent sitting beside the dying embers of campfires, dreaming of the ghosts who had once been part of his life. Then he gestured toward the door as he shouldered his document case and hunting bag. "I must be away, sir. I have powder and ball from your provisions and I thank you for your generosity. I know supplies are short here."

"I could hardly do less," Smith answered. He stood and followed John from the building. Once outside, he glanced to where two men stood, clearly waiting for John. It was the Canadian, Samuel Roy, and the Oneida called Owela. What company Lord MacNeil kept! "Your brother and Miss MacNeil, sir?" Smith asked suddenly.

"They are aboard *Rampant*," John answered, waving

to his companions as they approached. "I am confident of their safety aboard a British ship of war, Lieutenant Colonel."

"Let us be off, John," said Samuel. "I have waited for you all day here in great impatience. Where are Mack and Jamie?"

John smiled at his friend. He had known Samuel since they were both boys. An experienced woodsman of French and Miami blood, the young man had traveled with John many times through the years. Samuel had made his home on Pêche Island with John; in truth, they were nearly inseparable, bound together by the events that had shaped their lives at Fort Detroit years ago.

"They have stayed aboard the ship," said John. "Would you return there as well, Samuel? You could keep them company."

"No, no, John. I go with you," Samuel snorted. "I am not so easy to be rid of, eh? I have had enough of the ship for a while, my friend."

"He is no sailor, he tells me. He does not always have the stomach for it," teased Owela, who leaned on his musket and watched Samuel with amusement. He grinned at his friend, MacNeil. The British officer he only looked over carefully. Owela was tall and smoothly muscled. Oddly for an Oneida, his head was not shaved. His long, black hair was tied back and lay hanging down his back. His ears were pierced and silver earrings glinted in the sunlight.

"Think on it, Lord MacNeil," advised Smith. "Your ward and your brother. They are secure on board a

British warship on Lake Ontario, but once trouble starts you would not want them to be in the middle of a revolution. Send the pair of them home now until the British military has put down the uprising that must surely come."

"I will consider the matter given the possibilities of war. I would not place them in such circumstances unless I had no other choice. You may be certain of that, sir," John answered him. "I am, unfortunately, aware of the dangers."

"God speed then, Lord MacNeil," the officer said.

Smith watched the party cross the fort's yard. John turned once and lifted his arm in farewell, then they disappeared out through the gate. And once back inside the stone house, if Lieutenant Colonel Smith heard the desperate firing of the swivel gun mounted on the rail of *Rampant*, he gave it not a single thought.

◇ ◇

Two days later, John returned to hear the horrible news. Jamie and Mack were gone. Kidnapped. The sailors on the deck of the ship had seen it happen, but with the sailing boat and canoe gone, they had been powerless to help. Again and again the swivel gun had been fired until soldiers had rowed out to *Rampant*. A party from the ship and Fort Niagara's men had searched for Jamie and Mack, but there was not a decent tracker amongst them. They had lost the trail and returned empty-handed.

Now as he stood on the silent beach in the early morning, John stared up at the fort that loomed above him. He closed his eyes. Mack and Jamie. He could not lose them!

John had never married. There had been someone once, someone with whom he might have spent his life, but that had not happened. He had learned to value friendship greatly since it seemed that he was to live his life unwed. But then Jamie and Mack had come to him, as filled with excitement over Canada as he had once been. John's life had changed. His companions still meant as much to him, but Jamie and Mack meant even more. He loved them. They were his family, and they were more precious to him than life itself.

John hoisted a pack across his shoulders and picked up his musket. Samuel and Owela gathered up their gear. The military was unable to spare men to help him search further for Jamie and Mack, and so the three of them had to do it alone. They were short-handed at the fort, Smith had said in apology, and not even John's influence could change that.

Perhaps the colonials were correct, John thought. Perhaps the ties with Britain should be cut, whether it be for the sake of trade or taxes or lost children. He felt a bitterness well up inside him, which he choked down as he and his friends set out.

For an hour they separated and combed the beach and bluff, ranging up and down the river and climbing to the high ground that overlooked the lake. The sun burned the mist off the water. Arrows of geese flew overhead, calling to each other. They all met again just beyond Fort Niagara.

"There are two parties," said Owela, wiping the back of a hand across his damp brow. John nodded his agreement. "One is larger than the other. All wear moccasins."

"*Merci*, Jamie and Mack, for not wearing the buckled shoes that would have given you away. At least the hard soles would have left clear tracks," Samuel grumbled. "They counted upon being followed and so split up, did they not, John?"

John nodded. "One group has gone to the south, and the other follows the trade route to Albany, I would think. Either spot would be a good place to sell captives." He swore under his breath.

"What say you, John?" Owela asked. "Which of us will go where?"

They looked to John, whose head was bent over his musket. As he thought, he twisted the ring he wore on his smallest finger round and round. It was oddly shaped, a curl of silver that had been made long ago from the handle of an old spoon. He lifted his head and straightened. "Samuel and I will go south. It will be a hard search, I fear, Samuel."

"The search will not go nearly as hard as what I have in mind for the kidnappers when I catch them," Samuel assured him. "We will find Mack and Jamie."

"We will, or I shall never stop looking. Owela, you will follow the other trail that leads east. It is your country and you know it far better than we do." John reached under his shirt and pulled out a locket that hung on a ribbon around his own neck. He slipped it off and handed it to Owela.

The young Oneida pried it open. Within was a tiny painting, a miniature of a girl. Dark wing-like brows arched over blue eyes that stared frankly and seriously from her face. She did not smile, but a hint of something that might be mischief or even defiance lifted the corners of a wide mouth. It was a strong face with oval cheekbones nearly as high as his own. He snapped the locket shut and slipped the ribbon over his head. The locket dropped inside his shirt.

"Mack does not know about this locket. It was to be a surprise," John said to Owela. "In fact, she is not even aware that I painted her portrait. I meant to send it back to Brierly with the next packet of letters. It has been several years since they have seen her, you know." He gestured helplessly.

"Take heart, John," said Owela. "They will see her and your brother yet again."

John pulled the silver ring from his finger. "Mack has not met you, nor has Jamie. I think that they will never follow you back even with the locket as proof of who you are. But if they see this, they will be certain that I have sent you to them." And he pressed the ring into Owela's hand. Owela slipped it on his own little finger.

"This is my fault. I should not have left the two of them. If you find Mack and Jamie, Owela, do not leave their sides until I arrive," John said. His voice shook with emotion. "They are all I have. They are my heart's blood."

"I promise you I will," said Owela. Then with no more

talk — for what more could be said — John and his friends started out.

They hurried away from the fort. Even at this early hour, traders and Natives were entering the Gate of Five Nations and heading toward the Trade Room to do business there. Curious glances drifted over them, but no one dared to question the grim-faced party. John felt there was an air of decline about the place. The firm grip the British had here might just be loosening after all. But John did not want to think about that right now; there were other matters more important.

"If you find them too far to the east, do not try to return to Niagara," John said quietly to Owela as they walked. "Bad winter weather may come quickly and if we have storms, the traveling will be too hard for them. And there is this threat of revolution. Go instead to Boston if you can and send word to me somehow. You can shelter on my family's ship. It is the *Odonata* and it will be anchored in Boston harbor, or at one of the wharves, with Captain Apple and the crew onboard." He squeezed his friend's arm. "I leave it to your judgement, Owela."

"I do not know Boston at all," Owela answered doubtfully. "The woods, yes, the land between here and there, I know them well, but not this city."

"I have a friend there who has influence and you must seek him out," John said to Owela. "The ring and the locket will tell him who you are. He is a good man, a silversmith. His name is Paul Revere."

And so they parted. John and Samuel set off to the

south. And with the locket brushing warm and smooth against his chest within his shirt, and the silver ring on his finger like some precious talisman against evil, Owela turned east and began the hunt.

CHAPTER THREE

With Ben Sparks and his men, Mack and Jamie had disappeared within moments into the brush, and then, once away from the cleared area beyond the fort, into the deep woods.

Mack walked ahead of Jamie. Now and again she tried to look back to make certain he was keeping up, but when she did, the rope Sparks held chafed badly at her neck. There was no talking. Only the sounds of heavy breathing and footsteps crunching in the dry leaves met her ears.

Then there was a muffled crash and someone swore. Mack turned around to see Jamie on the ground, coughing and gasping as one of the men pulled on the rope to force him up. With both hands she grasped the thong looped about her own neck and jerked back on it with all her strength.

"For pity's sake, stop!" she screamed at Ben Sparks. "They are choking him!" He cursed at her and the burn she had given his hands, but released the rope. Mack ran back to Jamie and dropped to her knees beside him.

"I am fine," he said hoarsely.

"You are not," raged Mack as she turned on Sparks. "We are going with you. Is it too much to ask that we be treated decently?"

He jabbed his finger at her. "Watch your mouth, my girl. You are both mine and I will do what I wish with you. If you care so very much, help him yourself!" He instructed the men to remove the tethers. "But do not think of running. You will be shot if you do."

So Jamie and Mack walked together, hand in hand. Sometimes Jamie leaned a bit upon her for support. Sometimes she did the same, if only to assure him that he was at least as strong as her.

"We can do this," she would whisper to Jamie again and again. "We are strong enough to do this."

Over the next few days, they followed the trade route from Niagara along the lake to the Oswego River and then headed south. Always a man went on ahead to warn if any other parties were approaching. Sparks led them clear of homesteads, and although she sometimes caught the whiff of wood smoke from a chimney or campfire, Mack saw no other people.

Ben Sparks was clearly the leader. Neither of the other two kidnappers appeared to have names. Sparks gave orders in a low, angry voice, adding various insults, and they addressed each other in the same fashion.

"Pick up that pack, you piece of dirt," one would growl.

"Get it yourself, you fat dolt!" the other might respond.

"Quit fighting, you idiots!" Sparks would hiss, and for a while there might be peace between the men, or at least what passed for peace within this band of ruffians, but then it would start up again. There were low conversations by the fires. The army came up now and again; Albany or Boston were sometimes discussed. Oswego had been avoided since it was too close to Niagara, and their captives might have been recognized.

Camp was always a comfortless business, the fires small, the meat tastelessly cooked. Then the cook fire would be put out and a second cheerless camp set up some distance away in darkness, so that smoke from a fire might not lead anyone to them. They slept for only a few hours, it seemed to Mack, and then were prodded awake to march on yet another day, farther and farther from Niagara.

Jamie and Mack were now allowed to walk freely between the men. Thoughts of escape were far from their minds; they believed Sparks' violent threats and knew he would hunt them down should they run. Sparks did not even seem to care that they sought privacy when they had to go into the bushes. Mack would stand watch for Jamie, and he did the same for her.

"Such delicate manners they have, our fine prizes, don't you know," Sparks scoffed one quiet evening when they had emerged from the brush. The other men were checking their weapons and arguing between themselves as to who would take the first watch. They paid Ben little attention.

"He stares at you so," Jamie whispered in an angry tone. "It makes me sick to see it, Mack."

"It means nothing to me," Mack answered in a low voice, as she turned her face from Sparks. But she was conscious of the way he constantly watched her, as though he were making plans. She had no wish to know what those plans might be.

"Where can John be? Do you suppose he will ever be able to find us?" Jamie asked in a breathless whisper one night as they lay close together under the foul blankets Sparks had given them. Mack did not know, but she could not tell Jamie that. The thought of not being rescued terrified her, and each night her dreams were filled with awful images of what might happen in time. Still, she tried to lift up Jamie's lagging spirits.

"All will be well. Turn over, Jamie, and squeeze closer. We will soon be warm," she said in a comforting whisper. Her voice was as quiet as she could make it. "He will find us somehow."

"I can think of no way to leave a sign," whispered Jamie over his shoulder.

"I will think of something," soothed Mack. There was no answer. Exhausted by the walking and the tension, Jamie was fast asleep. She felt Jamie's warmth seep into her bones, and her eyes dropped shut.

Mack dreamed of John that night and of the small, stony rattle of the sheepshead stones he shook in his hand like dice from a freshwater sea. You must toss the dice and gamble, his ghostly voice said. When she woke in the morning as the men broke camp in darkness, she knew what she would do. There were more than a dozen sheepshead stones in her pouch. No one had touched the pouch. In fact, no one had touched either of them again since the day Jamie had fallen.

"No rough business with either of our chicks, you mangy pigs," Ben had growled to his followers. He turned his head and winked at Mack. "They're wearing fine English wools and they look like little gentlemen. At least, one of them does." Jamie made a small gagging noise.

That night in the darkness, when she was certain she would not been seen, Mack dropped a single stone onto the path they followed. I will do the same thing every night, she thought. The stone lay on the dried moss. To most eyes it would look like a tiny pebble or perhaps the slightly curving fragment of a bird's egg. Mack hoped that to someone who was following their trail, the stone would stand out as clearly as a sign posted in the forest. Follow this way, it would proclaim. Later, as they lay close together against the cold, she told Jamie what she had done. He grinned in the darkness.

"You are so clever, Mack. Surely John will find us quickly now," he whispered, with barely restrained excitement. "How ever did you think of it?"

"I dreamed it," answered Mack quietly, but she did not explain.

The next day it rained. A cold, soft drizzle misted the forest. Mack held the stinking blanket closely around herself, and she leaned forward as she walked, so that at least the front of her shirt would stay dry. She could not have the fabric wet and clinging to her bosom.

The rainy weather did not last, and for the next week a pale sun shone. Sparks pushed them hard and at the end of each day Mack and Jamie were exhausted. But in the quiet darkness, Mack was able to drop a stone from her pouch and so she took hope from that. Then one morning the men seemed to cheer, and although their insults and arguing continued, they took on an expectant air. Mack felt despair, for their excitement could only mean that at the very least Jamie would soon be sold.

They smelled the camp before they saw it that afternoon: sweating horses and their droppings, wood fires, and the sweet scent of roasting meat that dripped its sputtering fat from spits. Sparks led them over a slight rise to where soldiers camped in a clearing. The officers' tents were off in the distance, far from the common rabble of the troops. Men sat or lay about in groups like red-coated cardinals that had dropped to earth. Muskets stood stacked in threes, barrels pointing to the sky.

This was a very different army from the one Jamie and Mack knew at Fort Niagara or Detroit. Here there were no barracks, no stone buildings or magazines for ammunition and powder. This was the British military on the move.

Away from it all lay another camp quite different from that of the King's forces. This was a camp of civilians, although soldiers were there as well. Men and women sat on low stools or on the ground carrying on some small task or another, talking to the soldiers who mingled amongst them.

"Who are they?" asked Jamie, staring at the people.

"I have no idea," answered Mack in tired confusion. Why would any sane civilian wish to follow soldiers across country as rugged and unforgiving as this? She glanced nervously at the red uniforms. The thought that Jamie might find himself part of them caused a cramp of fear to grip her belly.

"It will be well," Jamie whispered softly as he squeezed her arm. "We will just tell them who we are."

"We have no proof that we do not belong to Ben Sparks," Mack groaned hopelessly. "He has no papers for us, but that will not matter. And when they learn I am female, I know it will be worse. Jamie, these men are not like John. This is the military."

"What are you whispering about, chickies?" hissed Sparks in Mack's ear, and she shrank from him. "Do not fear, Mack, I will not leave you here." He turned to Jamie. "You might not think so now, lad, but you will miss me and the fine way you have been treated. The King's boys will make you dance to a very lively tune indeed. Mack, my girl, you will stay close to me and not say a word." And for the first time since the day on the beach, he touched her, grasping her arm firmly.

"You are pond scum, Ben Sparks," she said to his face.

Sparks chuckled softly. "Why, thank you, Miss Mack," he whispered.

Sparks pulled Mack forward, down the gentle slope toward the clearing. Jamie stayed close by her side. The other two men followed, excited by the prospect of a sale and coins in their pockets. Every nerve in Mack's body cried out that she must pull away from Sparks and run, but her feet felt like stones as she stumbled on beside this man that she loathed.

A few eyes turned their way as they walked between

the rough tents, but most people kept to their tasks. One man was repairing a harness. A woman sat on a blanket, taking small stitches in the torn sleeve of a red coat. Two young girls sat together on the grass, their knitting needles clicking in their hands as they talked and gossiped together. Stockings, mittens, and sleeveless under-vests lay spread on display for sale around them.

If I were a man I would need one of those under my uniform this winter, thought Mack suddenly. Before she could stop herself, tired and worn from a forced march these endless days, she began to laugh aloud. It was a soft snorting at first, then a giggle, then loud, uncontrolled laughter. Jamie elbowed her. Who could say what effect this might have on Ben's mood? He still had time to shoot them or jab them with his knife. Ben Sparks' face grew a deep red. He dug his fingers painfully into her arm, but still Mack could not stop.

At the sound of Mack's laughter, a large woman straightened up from the pot she was stirring and stared at them. If she had not heard the sound, she would not have seen the group at all, so intent was she on seasoning the food she cooked. Molly Ladle squished her round face into a furious frown, straightened her ruffled cap upon her head, set her red, rough fists on her hips, and bellowed. "Ben Sparks, you worthless trash, I told you what I would do if I ever set eyes on you and your pack of rats again in my camp!"

Sparks winced. He had hardly expected to meet the woman here, since she usually traveled between Boston and Albany. He shoved Mack and then Jamie ahead of him and the group picked up their pace, but Molly moved quickly in spite of her size. She stopped Sparks in his tracks and shook her heavy iron ladle at him.

"Now, Molly, darling, don't be sticking your pretty nose where it doesn't belong," he cautioned.

"I am not your darling and my nose is about as pretty as an over-boiled carrot, so do not be trying those tricks on me!" growled Molly. She edged slowly toward him.

"Let me pass, woman," Sparks cried angrily.

"You shall not!" Molly roared. "And the two poor things you have this time for selling! You will not do it again. It makes me sick to think of all the children you and those dogs have stolen over the years. You will not do it again, I say!"

Molly swung her ladle with all her strength and brought it down onto Sparks' skull. He dropped to his knees in the grass, holding both hands to his head. Quickly moving away from him, Mack thought that it made a lovely sound. His men moved forward cautiously, muskets raised.

"You will be very sorry for that, Molly, darling," Sparks moaned as he struggled to his feet and carefully probed at his head. His hands came way, red with blood.

"Oh, I doubt she will," said a calm voice behind Mack.

A big, solid-looking man set down the bowl of stew he had been eating. He picked up the musket that lay close by his side and rose to his feet. From beneath the beaver felt hat he wore, his eyes glittered like cold stones. Then the soldier sitting near him did the same. One by one a dozen men stood and leveled their muskets at Ben and his followers.

"I was taken and sold into service as a boy," said an older soldier. "Was not fond of it myself."

"I was, as well," commented another. "Never saw my ma again." Slowly the soldiers moved toward Jamie and Mack. Someone pulled them out of the way, and a wall of red stood between them and their captors.

"Those two are mine!" shouted Sparks, dodging the ladle that Molly waved at him.

"Not now they are not," she said resolutely. "Now leave here, you beast! Will you march him and his rabble far from the camp, lads?" A few of the soldiers came forward with their weapons held ready.

"I swear that I am not finished with you yet," raged Sparks as he glared at Mack. "I do not give up what is mine, and doubt it not, you are mine. Our paths will cross again and it will not go pleasantly for you, my chick. I vow that." Sparks raised his clenched fist to her in a threat.

The big man who had first spoken stepped forward and set a hand on Mack's shoulder. "You have nothing to fear now," he said softly. His voice grew louder. "But I cannot say the same for you, Ben Sparks. Take care whom you threaten here. I would not like to think that my young friends might ever come to any harm at your hands. I promise you will pay a high price, indeed, if such an unfortunate thing happens, or, in fact, if I ever learn that you have taken another child to sell as a slave. Remember that well, Sparks."

Sparks said no more as he and his men left the camp. Mack knew that she should look away, but she could not help herself. She watched until Sparks and the others reached the edge of the forest. He turned then, and his eyes met hers with a silent vow that sickened her heart. He nodded once. Then he was gone.

"The soldiers will make sure that rabble is far from the camp. Those cowards will not be back," Molly declared, anger still in her voice. "And if they are fools enough to do so, then there is always this!" She shook the ladle in the air like the weapon it was. "I must wash it before I put it back in the stew, lest my fine food carry the taste of Ben Sparks' thick skull." She rinsed the ladle carefully with water from a pot that hung simmering over one of her fires, then she rubbed it dry with her apron. Back into the stew it went.

"Thank you," Mack offered simply. The relief she felt made her knees weak. She unclenched her hands and looked down at her palms. Even with her short nails, the marks of red half-moons showed on the skin, so hard had she been squeezing her fists.

"Are you hungry, lad?" asked the big man in the felt hat. He had filled a bowl with stew and offered it to Jamie.

"Thank you, sir," Jamie said and he sat in the grass and ate as Molly Ladle gave Mack a bowl. Taking it, Mack smiled her thanks at this woman who had saved them.

"I cannot pay you. We have no money," she said in a small voice between bites. She had just seen coins change hands as soldiers bought stew from Molly. The woman waved her rough hand in the air, brushing the idea away as she would a fly.

"To see that animal on the run was payment enough, was it not, Elias?" laughed Molly. "Besides, you are my guests, are you not? Have you names?"

"We are Mack and Jamie MacNeil," Mack introduced themselves.

"Ah!" said Elias. "Kin, then. And I wager you will have quite a story to tell us." There was a twinkle in his blue eyes, for he did love a good story.

"It will keep for later, Elias," scolded Molly. "Let the poor things eat."

They sat and talked in the late afternoon sunshine as soldiers came and went from Molly's fire. She was a camp follower and had been for longer than anyone could remember. They were an odd pair, Molly Ladle and Elias Stack, friends for many years.

Molly had loved a young British soldier many years ago and, against her parents' wishes, had followed him when the army left. They might have married in time, but the soldier was killed. Alone and far from home, her name ruined, unwelcome in the house of her father, she did what she must. She traded her silk petticoats for an iron pot and ladle. They became her weapons and her livelihood. She traveled along with one regiment or another and was well known for the tasty soups and stews she cooked. Few could recall what her surname had once been, though, and to them she was simply Molly Ladle.

It was in such a way that Elias Stack had met her years ago during the French and Indian War, one of a series of struggles between France and Britain over this continent. Then he had been a colonial militiaman. More than once Molly's food had warmed his belly on a cold night. Now with the wars over and all of Canada and the colonies in British hands, he was a trader. He was cheerful and jovial with a fine sense of humor. Vestiges of his past as a soldier still clung to him, though. The watchful way he moved told of a man who weighed the world about him with a calculating and learned eye.

"It is an honorable profession to follow the troops, and let none tell you otherwise," said Elias, spooning up the last of his stew and wiping his mouth delicately with the back of a large hand. "The sutlers give the men the things the army cannot." He smiled at Mack's confused expression. "Sutlers, my girl. They are the skilled folk who travel along with the army and serve the soldiers in many ways. Why, a fellow may not have the time or the desire to darn the holes in his socks or cook up his own dinner. There are those who will do it for him. For a price."

Molly held out her hand to a young soldier who had come to her fire. He dropped some coins into her palm, and she ladled out a bowl of steamy stew for him.

"It's good," he said to Molly as he ate, nodding his thanks. He only glanced at Jamie and Mack. "It's polecat tonight with the boys, and I cannot face that again."

"Now, lad, there is nothing wrong with a fat polecat," Molly told him, wiping her hands on her apron. "If you know how to cook it up proper, that is."

The young man ate noisily. "Well, they scorch it a bit and then you eat it. How sounds that?"

Jamie laughed out loud, but Mack kept her eyes and face turned away from the young man. She could feel his eyes on her, no doubt wondering who this strange girl was, but she had had enough attention for one day. Ben Sparks and his threats came into her mind. At the thought of him a wave of sickness rose up her throat.

"Well, send them over if they cannot stomach their meal. I have plenty of stew tonight."

"They are tougher than that, Molly. They would eat a cooked boot and think nothing at all if there was spruce beer to wash it all down," the soldier laughed. He stood up and wiped his mouth on his sleeve. Then, shooting another curious glance at Mack, he thanked Molly again and stalked away, his red coat flapping along his legs.

Mack said nothing but inwardly sighed with relief. Why had he watched her like that? She lifted her eyes to see that Elias now watched her as well. There was no menace in his look, though, only a thoughtful scrutiny. He nodded to himself and then broke into an open smile that changed his face.

Mack felt the food move from her belly into her blood. Her fingers and her feet felt thick and warm in the cool air. They had not eaten so well since they had been dragged away from the ship at Fort Niagara. She looked across the fire at Jamie to see him drooping.

"A sleep will do you both good." Elias slapped his thighs.

"That it will, Elias," Molly answered, and she gestured toward her tent. Its canvas was old and stained with years of travel, but the blankets that lay neatly folded inside were clean and, as Mack soon learned, smelled of dried mint leaves, which were sprinkled within their wool folds.

"I cannot ever thank you enough for this," Mack said

to Molly as they entered the tent. Molly drew the tent flaps down and busied herself spreading blankets.

"No reason to, my girl," she answered. "There were those who helped me long ago when I was alone. I can do no less for someone in need." She shook a blanket over Jamie who, overcome by the hot food, exhaustion, and the sheer relief at their deliverance, rolled over into a ball. A mutter of thanks came from him. Then Molly turned to Mack and crossed her arms over her considerable bosom.

"So, now tell me, my girl, how is it you have been wandering about on your own in a man's breeches?"

CHAPTER FOUR

Mack carefully watched Molly's face, her heart pounding within her chest. She saw no threat there, and the expression in Molly Ladle's eyes held only a kind warmth.

"I think you have been through much this last while," Molly went on gently. "I did not think you wished to talk of it in the open."

"I did not," Mack said in a trembling voice. "I have thanked my stars that I was dressed this way when Ben Sparks took us. I cannot imagine what might have happened had I been in skirts."

They sat in the tent with Jamie dozing quietly between them, and Mack told Molly everything. The woman shook her head. She set one hand on Jamie's limp shoulder and brushed the hair out of Mack's eyes with the other. Then she drew the back of her rough hand down Mack's cheek.

"You will stay with us," Molly said firmly.

"We cannot," Mack argued, her voice desperate. "I must get Jamie back to Niagara. Surely, we look enough like a pair of boys that we will not be bothered. Perhaps we may travel by night."

"Why, it is clear to anyone who has eyes to look," Molly laughed. "No man might say you are a pretty lass, but pretty does not always tell the story."

The ribbon had slipped from Mack's hair and the dark waves hung to her shoulders. She was tall and slim, this girl, with wide shoulders and, beneath the wool breeches, a lean form made leaner by her recent ordeal. In time she would fill out as all young girls did, and then how the heads would turn, Molly thought. For now her face, with its serious eyes and set mouth, the cheekbones pink with the crisp air, was only interesting.

"You need not fear for yourself or him, Mack. We shall watch for you. My old friend, Elias Stack, will see to it. He may be trusted to keep you safe."

"He did seem to loathe the idea of our being sold," mused Mack in tired confusion. "Was he sold himself?"

"No," Molly told her. "He was not ever sold, but having been taken prisoner by the French during the French and Indian War, he detests the idea of captivity." She shook her head and sighed. "He escaped but has no love for the French. They destroyed all he had when they took Oswego."

"He is a sutler then, like you are?"

"Not our Elias Stack. A trader in furs he is, working down in the town of German Flats. Now and again we meet when he is traveling between the Mohawk and Niagara."

"Niagara!" whispered Mack in excitement. "He knows the way there. We must return to the fort!"

Molly heaved herself to her feet, smoothed her skirts and apron, and shook her head. "Sleep now. All that will be talked about soon enough. You may not know it, but you are fair worn-out."

She truly was. Mack rolled herself in a blanket and leaned into Jamie's warm back. The sun had been low in the sky when they came into the tent. The canvas walls were tinted pink with the coming sunset. For the first time in days she felt herself relax. She did not have to think about armed and dangerous men who slept a stone's throw away or wonder what was snapping and rustling in the night. She sighed and buried her face against Jamie. They would get home somehow, no matter what she must do.

When Mack woke, she was alone. Soaked in sweat, she had been dreaming of Ben Sparks. She might have sat up straight in panic, but the smell of the canvas and old mint-scented wool blankets brought her gently to her senses. Mack lay stiff and still for a moment, until her breathing quieted and her racing heart slowed. Surely I have slept for hours, she thought. All was dark, although Mack could see patches of what must be firelight glowing faintly through the canvas. She sat up and pushed aside the blanket. There were voices and laughter outside. Nearby, someone tuned a fiddle, and notes from a fife sounded sweetly.

Mack stood and pulled her clothing into place. She picked up her wrinkled ribbon from where it lay in the nest of blankets and, dragging her fingers through her hair, tied it back at her neck. Pushing aside the tent flaps, she stepped out.

A change had come over the camp. It was not just the darkness and the fresh night air. Pine knots popped in the fires, sending sparks into the sky. Like the ghosts of fireflies, they wavered up and melted away. People stood or sat in groups, but now there was no business being done. Stone jugs were passed from hand to hand, and Mack caught the sharp tang of whiskey fumes and pipe tobacco. Soldiers had come into the sutlers' camp. Couples strolled from fire to fire or stood just beyond the light in quiet conversation. Someone called for music and only the sentries who walked the encampment's perimeters, or stood sharp-eyed with muskets in their hands, gave any thought to what may wait beyond in the darkness.

"Mack!" called Jamie from where he sat by a fire with Molly and Elias.

Mack made her way over to them, weaving in and out of the people.

"Had a good rest, did you?" asked Elias. He looked her over critically. "Fresh and ready for the evening, I do think, miss."

"Indeed, sir," replied Mack. "Molly was correct. I was quite worn-out."

She looked around the encampment. Couples were now joining hands and standing in four pairs to make a square. There will be dancing, thought Mack in surprise. It was the last thing she expected to see in this place.

"Yes, they like to dance on a Saturday evening," Molly said in response to Mack's surprised expression. "If it is quiet and safe, mind you. Takes a person's thoughts off of the hardships, you know. These men have been far from home for a long while."

An older soldier with a fiddle stood off to the side. A very young boy stood near him, a fife in his hands; he would play marches for the army as a rule. How young he is, thought Mack. Had he been sold into this as Jamie nearly had? A shiver ran down her to think how close Jamie had come to that fate.

The two heads leaned together, one touched with gray, the other fair. They spoke to each other softly, the soldier counted out a beat, and then they began to play. Someone called the figures as the dancers moved to the lively music. Familiar tunes, first "Corn Riggs," then "Morgan Megan" spilled out into the night. Then the fiddler and the young fifer began a brisk version of "The Handsome Cabin Boy."

"Will you dance with me, sir?" A young girl stood in front of Jamie. "You do look like a handsome cabin boy yourself." She reached out and, grasping his hand, boldly pulled him across the clearing. The look on his face was so startled that Mack laughed out loud. Jamie's neck, then his cheeks, and then his ears turned a bright red.

"And you with me, sir?" whispered a teasing voice just behind Mack. She turned around to see another young woman, her hand held out in invitation. "If you are a lad, then so am I. I'll not ask why you are dressed this way, if you'll dance with me." Then she went on loudly, "I will not drag you about like my sister, Meg, has done your friend. Besides, I am a better dancer."

"You'll have to prove that to your partner, Liza," called her sister, who had already pulled Jamie into the dancers. Mack opened her mouth to refuse, for how could she do such a thing? But Molly, knowing what she was about to say, gave her a push.

"Off you go," shouted Elias with a great rumble of laughter as Mack was led away. "Dance up a storm! Meg and Liza are both fine girls. You will have to decide for yourself who is the better dancer, though!" Mack looked back to see Elias wiping his streaming eyes as his shoulders shook with amusement. Then with two other couples they formed a set and the dance began.

Mack bowed gracefully, thankful for the times she had watched John or Jamie do the same, and then she held Liza's hands. Yellow curls peeped out from under the lace-trimmed cap that covered the girl's head. Her brown eyes shone with the evening's excitement and her cheeks flushed prettily. As the music played, they began a series of figures, patterned moves, first with each other and then with another couple, Jamie and Meg.

"You are a fine dancer, my boy," Jamie shouted to Mack. Then, as he passed her, he whispered, "If you could see the expression on your face!"

"Thank you, kind sir!" answered Mack. Changing partners, she leaned close to Jamie's head and threatened, "I shall joyfully strangle you later!" But it was in good fun, and Mack found herself laughing as the figures were repeated with another couple and then another. When the music stopped, they were all damp with perspiration in spite of the chilled air.

Mack was conscious of her own rich scent, her unwashed hair, and travel-worn clothing. There had been little chance to wash or to clean their teeth when they had been with Sparks. How fine a scrub, even one in cold water, would have been. How lovely it would have been to peel off the dirty clothing and wash away that awful journey.

There was no time for that, it seemed. The music was starting again, and her partner would not release her hand. They danced on, stopping now and again so that the fiddler and fifer could take refreshment and the dancers might regain their wind. Then, as suddenly as it had begun, the evening was over. People were drifting away into the darkness like the season's last moths. Soldiers headed to their tents. The old fiddler and the boy wandered back to their encampment, and the forest's silence settled around them once more.

"We will strike camp as soon as the sun rises," said Molly, "and you girls should get to your beds." Meg and Liza each bobbed a quick curtsy. Jamie and Mack made short bows. Elias watched the two sisters with his sharp eyes. When they were within their own tent he turned to Mack and Jamie.

"You will sleep safely here," Elias said to them in a kind voice, "for I will be just outside." He picked up his blanket roll that lay near the tent. Bidding a good night to them, he shook out his blanket and made up a bed, his loaded musket within close reach.

Molly, Mack, and Jamie went inside the tent. "Tomorrow I will find some fresh clothing for you,"

Molly said. "And I will wash your dirty shirts and breeches when we make camp. You are a bit ripe, you know, especially after the dancing. I can do nothing with your coats, but the rest can be improved." She wrinkled her nose at them.

"Burning would improve them," suggested Jamie brightly.

"I suspect it would, lad," Molly answered. She shook out the old blankets and made up three beds. "Those are fine English woolens you are wearing, and it would be a shame to lose them. You will need warm clothing when the cold comes."

"I hope we are safely back with John before that happens," Jamie said. "Are you certain Ben Sparks will not return?"

Molly kicked off her shoes, loosened her stays, and pulled off her cap, then sank onto the ground. "We are ready if he does. Who might say what can happen in the night, what nasty criminal might come creeping back to snatch up the prizes he has lost? My ladle is close by, Elias Stack is just outside, and we will keep you poor things from danger."

Jamie and Mack pulled off their moccasins and sat down upon the blankets. Mack folded the rough fabric into pleats with her fingers, then took a deep breath for courage.

"We are in your debt, but we cannot spend the winter here. We must get back to Fort Niagara," she said quietly. "John will be sick with worry."

"Well, a person may not just wander off into the

forest," Molly stated practically while she settled herself for the night. Pulling the pins from her hair, she began to braid a thick plait. "It would be no small task to find your way home again alone."

"We can try," said Jamie. He pulled the scratchy blanket up to his chin. Outside, the sounds of the camp settling for the night could be heard. A dry branch cracked as a sentry walked his rounds, a woman laughed in the distance, and the wind made a rushing sound in the great oaks that stood around them.

"No," Molly said in a stern voice as she lay herself down, squirming to find a comfortable spot. "It is too far and too much of a risk. Sleep now. It will wait until tomorrow."

Mack pulled up her blanket and curled herself into a small shape. Jamie rolled close to her, seeking her warmth. She listened to his breathing and the breathing of Molly on her other side. She had been reckless before and thought nothing of it. To slip away in the sailing boat and play for an hour was a small thing compared to finding their way back to Niagara with no one to guide them. What if they ran into Ben Sparks? Mack's throat grew dry at the thought of what might happen to her then.

And then there was Jamie. Mack turned on her side and pushed at his shoulder. With a soft grunt he rolled over and she put her arm over him. She felt the keen sting of responsibility. No matter what, she would see him home again, Mack thought tiredly, and she fell asleep to the thunderous snores of Elias Stack rumbling in the night outside the tent.

They broke camp at dawn. There was much work to do, striking the tent and folding it, and then tying it and the kettles securely on Molly's packhorse. They wrapped blankets around themselves against the sharp air and, in the pale light of sunrise, ate a hasty breakfast as they worked. There would be stops along the way, but it would not be until evening that hot food could be prepared.

A half dozen sutlers followed the marching soldiers. It was a long day, but the size of the group kept the pace to one that Mack found easy. She was able to walk beside Elias and in hushed tones she told him what had happened to them, although she was certain Molly had already done so.

"You were lucky," Elias said slowly. "Ben Sparks held you in high regard." He smiled at Mack's shocked look.

"He treated us no better than a bag of wheat he might sell at market," Mack scoffed. "Why this horse might have meant more to him." She stroked the muzzle of Molly's horse as she walked alongside the animal. It blew softly into her hand and nickered in pleasure.

Elias laughed at such nonsense. "No. He valued you very highly. Jamie was coin in his pocket, and Sparks is not the sort of man to put up with losing a single coin. As for you, Miss Mack, I saw he had other plans, but they will never come to pass. Do not worry yourself."

Mack could not put it from her mind. She felt a crawling fear, but with it a growing anger. How dare that man lay his hands on them. How dare he think that he might own her!

When a halt was called for the evening, Molly quickly unpacked her pots and saw to her horse while Elias pitched the tent. Mack and Jamie set out to gather wood.

"You start the fires, Elias, my friend," Molly commanded when they returned. He dug a striker from his hunting bag and, with dried grass as tinder, soon had small flames on which he set the wood. Molly hung the kettles of water to boil. Then she disappeared among the other sutlers' tents. When Molly returned, the pots were bubbling. She was carrying shirts, stockings, and breeches.

"These belonged to two poor lads who drowned last spring," she explained. "We never throw anything away here amongst us. Who can say when it might be used?

"You may go to the stream to bathe if you wish, and here are willow twigs for cleaning your teeth," she said to Jamie. "Mack will wash inside the tent."

Jamie wandered off, a sliver of soap in his hand, a coarse towel slung over his shoulder. Mack ladled hot water into a bucket and went into Molly's tent with the clean garments. She pulled off her clothes and passed them out between the tent flaps to Molly. She washed her hair and her body with a piece of soap, and then dried herself with a rough, scratchy towel. It felt wonderful. She cleaned her teeth carefully and dressed. When Mack emerged from the tent carrying the pail of dirty water, Jamie was there with Molly and Elias. Their clothing simmered in the big pot to which another bit of soap had been added.

"You look nearly normal." Jamie eyed Mack's dripping hair and clean face.

"It does feel better," Mack answered. "Was the stream cold? That icy water would be a dreadful shock." She watched Molly pull the steaming clothing from the pot and set it on a nearby rock to cool.

"The shock of the water was nothing compared to the shock of knowing I was being watched," Jamie said grumpily. "I am certain I heard giggling coming from the bushes." Both Mack and Molly exploded in laughter.

"Perhaps your dance partner followed you," Elias said with a straight face. "If we find her in a dead faint in the bushes, we will know the truth."

"It would serve her right," Jamie answered. "Perhaps a bear will eat her."

In truth he gave little thought to whether he had been seen or not. In the small cabins on the ship there was often no room for that sort of modesty. He had only meant to make Mack laugh, and he felt a glow of happiness that he had done so. She had looked so worried and strained these last two weeks. He felt the need to protect her. As a young woman she was his responsibility, after all.

"A bear would choke on one of the Cooper lasses," observed Molly cheerfully. "Here, you two, take this clothing and rinse it in the stream. Then wring it and we will hang it on sticks near the fires to dry."

There was no festive air that evening. Soldiers came and went for food, and the camp settled into itself for the night. Mack caught more than one curious look cast their way.

"We must try to return to Niagara," she repeated to Molly late that night. Most of the camp was quiet. Only a few people sat out by their fires here and there. "They must be searching for us, and if we go farther from the fort, it will only make it harder for John."

"I suppose you must," Molly replied thoughtfully as she and Elias drew on their pipes. It was a habit she had taken up over the years, not so ladylike perhaps, but then she was no lady when it came down to the facts of the matter.

"You are certain we can find the way back?" asked Jamie. He leaned forward to warm his hands at the fire. "Back to Fort Niagara, Mack?"

"No, my lad, you would not get there on your own." Elias looked up into the night sky. "This land seems empty but there are people everywhere, Native villages, and homesteads up and down the entire way. There are criminals, too, as you well know." Molly nodded. She drew on the clay pipe and sent a drift of smoke puffing into the still air.

"We have to try," Mack insisted. She moved to put her arms about Jamie and rest her chin on the top of his head as she often did on the ship, then she stopped. She planned to pass herself off as a boy and so could do no such thing. A prickle of nervousness shot through her. How could she think to succeed with such a foolish plan? Any small thing might give her away to even those who did not look closely.

"Ah, the stubbornness of youth," said Elias. He blew a thin stream of smoke into the air and heaved a great sigh. "It would make more sense to go on to Albany. We are only a day from there. But I see you will have none of that. I must take you back to Fort Niagara myself then, it seems."

"We cannot ask you to do that," Mack said.

Elias held up a hand and silenced her. "You have not asked. I have offered. I would not sleep well knowing you were wandering aimlessly. The journey will not be an easy one and I will insist we go quickly, but I may scarcely leave you to stumble about the woods on your own." He stood. "Here. Into the tent with you." They followed Elias and Molly inside.

"You will put this tomahawk through your belt in the morning, young Jamie, and there it will stay," Elias told him.

"And you, Miss Mack, will keep this on your person," Molly said. She pulled a pistol out from her pocket and held it out to Mack.

"You know how to load and shoot this weapon?" asked Elias.

"I do indeed, sir. John insisted that I learn to do so, although I never thought I might need such a skill."

"It is an excellent skill for any woman to have," Molly assured her. "You shall do very well. I do hope you will not need to use it, though." Molly patted Mack's shoulder. "I will make certain you have warm blankets and food and such. With any luck, the snow will hold off," she added.

Mack could barely speak her thanks to Molly Ladle. "You have done so much for us already. How can we repay you?" she asked for what seemed the hundredth time.

"No need, my young friends," Molly chuckled, turning to follow Elias out into the darkness. She stopped at the tent's doorway and shook her finger at them. "Just recall this night if you ever meet with another such as yourselves. There is always someone who might want a kind act or a friendly word to help them along. Now, try to get some rest." The tent flap dropped after her, and Elias and Molly sat once more by the fire to finish their pipes and think of long ago when they had been young themselves.

"We are going home," Mack said to Jamie as they made up their beds. "I can scarcely believe it."

"This is nearly over," Jamie whispered. In the privacy of the tent, they threw their arms around each other and sighed with relief.

CHAPTER FIVE

Owela padded soundlessly through the forest, his eyes flicking from the oaks and hickories and leafless bushes in the distance to the ground and back again. He had found another one of the sheepshead stones yesterday. He had seen such stones before on the lakes when traveling in the north with his father. Some people made earrings with them. Others carried them in their medicine bags for luck. Yesterday he had leaned down in the afternoon light to see the small disk of bone on the forest floor. It had been placed there by someone as a sign. He was certain of that.

"Who has put you there?" he asked the stone, picking it up and rolling it between his palms.

It had to be John MacNeil's brother and the girl. He could feel it in his blood as surely as he knew he was close to them now. There had been a day or so where the trail followed that of the army, but then it looped around. And now there were only three sets of tracks leading back to the west, following a path that was slightly away from the trade route. What sort of trouble might that mean?

Owela was a good tracker. The British had offered him silver more than once to scout for them, but he had no wish to deal with the military any more than he must. So many promises had been made to his people, the Oneida and other tribes, and so few kept. Like his father, Alex Doig, he had learned a mistrust of the redcoats.

As he picked his way along the path, he shifted the musket, bow, and quiver of arrows he carried. The weapon was loaded and ready to fire should danger come. He thought often of his father during these days alone in the wilderness. Owela was a full-blooded Oneida, as was his mother. His natural father had died in the war between the French and English when Owela was just a small child. Then, one fall, seven years ago, four men had come to trade at Oneida Castle, the village of Owela's people. One was John MacNeil. Wallace Doig and Natka were with him. The last was one of Wallace's sons, Alex, a young man of Scots and Miami blood. With his black hair that hung braided down his back and his lilting accent, Alex was unlike anyone Owela had ever met. John and his friends returned to Fort Detroit, but Alex stayed behind. By the summer Alex was married to Ní:ki, the mother of Owela. It did not take long for her son to love his new father greatly, even breaking Oneida tradition to look more like him.

"You are Oneida!" teased the other boys. "Why will you not pluck the hairs from your head as we do? And you have barely any tattoos!"

"I have enough," Owela answered. "My father has his

hair and I keep mine." But the taunting had always been good-natured, the sort of thing that boys everywhere do to torment each other. Now, at seventeen years, he was a man amongst his people, and no one teased him any longer.

Owela stopped for a moment and listened as crows flew overhead, lazily swooping. Their cries rang in the air and then they were gone. It had become a challenge to him, this hunt; it was days before he was certain the trail he followed was theirs. The sheepshead stones convinced him of this. He did not know these people, this Mack and the boy, Jamie, but he had heard of them from John. Each night as he sat quietly alone, the deep darkness of the woods pushed away only a little by the moon and stars, he slipped the locket from within his shirt and popped it open. The silver felt warm in his hand, a strange counterpoint to the cool eyes that looked out from the portrait.

What sort of female was she, this Mack? He would know soon enough — he could hear careless voices in the distance. He shifted the musket in his arms and shrugged his shoulders to more comfortably settle the bow and quiver of arrows, then he cautiously went on. He must take care not to surprise them.

Just ahead, Mack, Elias, and Jamie had stopped for the evening. They had been walking for two days now, and although he usually moved quite quickly through the forest, Elias had been considerate of the young people. They had tried their best to keep up without complaining, but they were tired now, and so he had called an end to the journey today sooner than he might have otherwise.

Elias chose a spot near a rocky ledge that overlooked the river, which would give them some protection from the wind. Mack stared tiredly at the bleak scene. Leaving her and Jamie to set up camp, Elias prepared to scout out the area as was his habit. He would return shortly; meanwhile, they were safe and hidden here. In a moment, the heavy brush and large trees blocked him from their view.

"How can John enjoy spending all this time in the woods, hunting his own food, sleeping on the ground? Nothing we have ever done with him has been so wretched. He has always seen that we were warm and comfortable on the ship or when we slept out in a camp in the forest. Until now I had no idea what a hard life he has lived here," Mack said to Jamie as she set their blankets and packs out of the way. Although she had loved the freedom of this land, the past two weeks with Ben Sparks and now this hurried journey home with Elias had shown her a harder side. Mack knew she could never live this way, given a choice.

"Well, John must travel if he is to see the country," said Jamie with a short laugh. "I do not like the ground part, but I do not mind the travel, although, my word, it is not leisurely, is it? I cannot say I would much enjoy being here alone, though. John has done it with his companions all these years. Things are always more of a pleasure when you share them with friends." Mack shivered a little. To go through this alone would have been impossible.

"Well, I cannot think of a friend who could persuade me to do it again!" she said firmly.

She picked up the small cook pot Molly had given them and turned to the river for water. Jamie was a dozen steps away, his arms filled with sticks. Behind him, the sunset glowed pink through the lacy branches of the trees. There were no sounds really, only their footsteps in the fallen leaves and the slight gurgle of the river where it tumbled over a rock.

Then she heard it. A low growling began behind her. Mack slowly turned. There, on the rock ledge, the sunset gleaming on its bared teeth, crouched a huge mountain lion. Every muscle was knotted in anticipation of movement. Its ears were held flat against its broad head, its tail lashed from side to side, and its muzzle wrinkled with each snarl.

"Do not move, Jamie," Mack whispered without looking at him. She slowly lowered the pot to the ground. The lion screamed.

"I would not think of it," answered Jamie weakly. Mack could hear the sticks rattling in his arms.

She carefully pulled the pistol from her belt. I can do this, she thought. I can do it! Slowly, slowly, she raised the pistol, never once taking her eyes from the lion until the weapon was aimed directly at the animal. The lion growled, then hissed, and bared its fangs.

"I would not do that," said a steady voice from off to the side. "The lion has only come to drink, you see, and you are between it and the water."

Mack's head snapped around at the sound of the soft

voice. A young Native stood there, legs braced, his musket pointed at the lion. Suddenly the lion leaped from the rock. Mack heard the scrabbling of claws and the heavy thump as it landed in the leaves and raced away. She turned so that she now pointed the pistol at the stranger, and he did the same, swinging his body around with an easy grace.

"Leave us," she said bluntly, trying to sound braver than she felt. "We want no trouble, sir."

Owela squinted his eyes and stared hard at Mack, then he glanced at Jamie. Surely this could not be the pair — oh, the boy perhaps, but not this great angry creature who stood facing him with eyes as dangerous as those of the lion that had just fled. "I am but passing by in search of someone. Perhaps you have seen them," he started to explain, but was suddenly interrupted.

"Stand off, my young fellow," Elias said in a silky tone. He had returned to the camp assured that all was uneventful and quiet only to find this scene. His musket was aimed at the intruder, and he stood calm and ready to fire.

Owela's eyes moved to the big man, but he did not answer him. "Would you be Jamie MacNeil and Mack?" he asked, turning his attention back to them. "If you are, it is good news and you may all lower your weapons. If you are not, then I ask that you lower them anyway, so I may go my way in peace."

"I have held these sticks long enough." Jamie dropped the bundle with a clatter. "How is it you know those names?" He crossed to Mack's side.

"John MacNeil searches for his kin," said Owela as he watched Mack warily. "He and a companion are following one trail. I have been following another. I would be pleased to know I have found you, but I have no wish to be shot."

"How can I know for certain you are who you say?" Mack asked him. She did not care for this strange young man with his haughty air.

"I will show you, but I must lower my musket and I will not do so as long as you are both pointing your weapons at me."

Mack's arm was beginning to tremble from the weight of the pistol. "Very well," she said shortly and she dropped it to her side.

Owela lowered his musket as Elias did the same. Then Owela pulled the silver ring from his finger and tossed it across the distance that separated him from Mack. The rays of the setting sun turned its circle of silver to a dull rosy glow. Mack caught it.

"It is John's ring!" Jamie said excitedly. "Yes, we are Jamie and Mack, and this is Elias Stack. I knew John must be searching for us! Is he far behind you? Where is Samuel?" Jamie stopped and blinked. "And who are you?"

"I am Owela of the Oneida people. I cannot say for certain where John and Samuel are, but you need not fear. They will find us. Until then, I have given my word that I will keep you safe." Owela looked at the boy and then grinned mischievously. "Though I think you have done well enough for yourselves." He glanced over at

Mack, who was just slipping the ring on her own finger, a small frown on her face.

"There is no need for that. We are with Elias," she said as politely as she could. "I would prefer you find John and tell him we are on our way to Niagara. I think you should leave immediately. Go, please, sir."

Owela shook his head. "I will do no such thing, miss," he said with a hint of irritation in his voice.

"Now, now, now," Elias soothed, seeing how the sparks flew between the two of them. "We shall talk of this once we are settled here."

They finished setting up camp and lit a fire. Jamie rambled on, telling Owela of Ben Sparks and how they had been taken. It was not until they had eaten and sat around the low flames that Mack spoke. Firelight flickered against the rock wall, and animals moving furtively through the undergrowth could be heard in the darkness. Mack carefully cleared her throat.

"I must apologize," she said to Owela stiffly. "I would not have held a pistol against you if I had known that John had sent you."

Owela cleared his own throat before speaking. Was there something wrong with their voices? Jamie wondered. He and Elias had watched the two of them all evening, carefully stalking around each other, clearing their throats now and again.

"It is nothing and I do accept your apology," Owela replied. He looked across at Elias, who nodded his agreement. "You were wise to be careful with a stranger who came upon you as I did."

Warned a thousand times by Jane that it was impolite to stare, Mack still could not keep her eyes from Owela. He was stretched out near the fire, warming his moccasined toes. He had taken off the hunting coat he wore, and he did not seem to feel the cold at all. With the sleeves of his shirt pushed up to the elbows, she could see the fine tattoos, long triangles and lines that patterned his forearms. Delicate blue zigzags ran along the brown skin of his jawbone. His bow, quiver, and musket leaned against the rock wall close by him, but he still wore his other weapons. One knife hung in a sheath around his neck, another from the belt at his waist. Mack cleared her throat again. She definitely must be getting a cold, Jamie thought.

"You tracked them all this way," Elias said suddenly, from where he lounged by the fire. "And yet when you found them, you doubted who they were?"

"Yes," Jamie added, tossing another thick stick onto the fire. "How many sets of people fitting our description could be wandering the woods?"

"That was the problem," answered Owela slowly. "You, I could be sure of, but not her. I had only this to help me and as you see, it does not look much like her." And, reaching inside his shirt, he grasped the silver locket and pulled the ribbon over his neck. He leaned over and passed it to Jamie. He popped it open.

"John has painted you!" Jamie exclaimed. "Did you know?" He crawled over and leaned close to Mack and they both examined the miniature. She smiled to think of John doing this picture, bent over the oval with his paints and tiny brushes.

"No, I did not," she answered softly. "How like him to do something like this and not say a word." She brushed a finger across the image.

Owela stared at Mack's downcast eyes, the lashes resting like shadows just above her cheeks. Her hair was loose upon her shoulders, and the campfire shot its waves with buttery light. Her mouth tilted in a smile. For just an instant he could see the same face that was in the painting. How that brief smile changed her. Then she snapped the locket shut and handed it back to him. The fixed, cold expression was back on her face.

"I have thanked heaven for weeks that I do not look like that, sir," she said stiffly. She suspected that he thought she was plain and boyish compared to John's lovely portrait, and that was somehow hurtful. She had never cared before. "I might not be alive today, nor Jamie, had I looked differently."

Owela was confused. What had he said? He did not know the girl and yet it seemed he had insulted her. "It is a good disguise," he said lamely as he poked unnecessarily at the fire with a stick.

Mack pulled her legs up to her chest and sat staring at the flames. She looked over at Elias. "It shall serve me well on the journey home to Fort Niagara and the ship. Elias is taking us there." She glanced coldly at Owela. "Tomorrow you must set out to find John and tell him we are on our way. I do insist upon this."

"You insist upon this? I am hardly under your orders, miss. And you will not be returning to Niagara," said

Owela quickly, bracing himself for her anger and feeling his own. Elias lifted his brows in surprise. Owela looked over at him. "There is the matter of this Ben Sparks. We are armed, but who can say how many men he may gather around himself? John MacNeil left the choice to me. He has said that I should take them to Boston. He has a friend there in that city and through him I will get a message to John that these two are both safe." Owela looked up at the sky. "And the weather will change for the worse at any time. I think it may snow tomorrow."

"There it is then," said Elias. "It seems I must place you in this fine fellow's hands. If you are willing, that is." There was only the slightest hint of menace in his voice, the unspoken threat of what might happen should any misfortune come upon either of them.

"It is John's wish," Owela answered Elias in the same tone. "I know he will thank you, sir, for how you helped them."

Elias, long accustomed to judging men, quickly liked what he saw. They would be fine with Owela. "I will go on to Niagara myself. I have friends along the way who will watch for John MacNeil and his companion. Word travels quickly here."

"I have no wish to go to Boston," Mack argued. She would not go with this Owela and neither would Jamie.

"If it is what John has decided, then we must go," Jamie said to Mack. "We can stay on board the *Odonata*. It is moored there, after all." How good it would be to see the great ship again, to talk with the crew, to stay in a familiar place once more.

"And your brother will join you there," Owela said to Jamie. There was no sense in speaking to the girl. She would be nothing but trouble on the trail, he suspected, but he had no wish to anger her further. "Perhaps he will take you back to England, instead of to Niagara."

Mack felt herself stiffen. This was too much. England! They had nearly been sold into servitude and now she was headed for slavery of another sort — the slavery of English society and fine china, of crystal goblets and the empty conversation of white-wigged gentlemen leaning over her hand. For even a little while it would be torture. And to be reminded of such a thing by this arrogant lout who sat across from her! She said nothing more, but Jamie could feel her rage burning above the heat of the fire.

"Sleep well, then." Owela pulled on his hunting coat and lay down next to the fire. Jamie stood and fetched the blankets for Elias, Mack, and himself. He started to shake his out, then stopped. Jamie walked round the fire and spread it over Owela, who sat up in surprise.

"I have no idea how you will be able sleep like that, on the ground, uncovered," Jamie said. "You will freeze. Mack and I shall share one blanket. You must use the other." As Owela opened his mouth to protest, Jamie went on, "You have helped us. If we are to continue on together, then we will share what we have with you."

Mack said nothing. Instead, she found the most comfortable spot she could near the rock wall, covered herself with her blanket, and turned her back on Owela. She pulled the blanket nearly over her head. Jamie squeezed in next to her for her warmth.

Owela lay there, his eyes open. He had lived with few possessions all his life; a little cold air meant nothing to him. He caught a slight smell of mint from the wool. The English girl must have her fine comforts, he supposed. He shook off thoughts of her and settled himself for sleep. Just as he was drifting off, he heard a breathy whisper from Jamie, who still faced him.

"She does, you know," came Jamie's low voice.

"She does what?" Owela whispered back.

"She does look precisely as John has shown her in that painting when she wears a gown." Then Jamie, too, fell silent and Owela was left alone with his thoughts and the soft, knowing chuckles of Elias Stack.

CHAPTER SIX

In the morning Mack spoke only when Elias or Jamie addressed her. Owela did not say a word to her, and she had nothing at all to say to him. There were rings under her eyes. She looked weary and drawn. She had dreamed of Ben Sparks again last night. Wakened in the dark by the vision of his cruel smile and hard eyes, she lay staring at the sky for hours until the sun rose.

"I will find John MacNeil, Miss Mack," Elias assured her, rolling his blanket and packing his gear. He set his felt hat on his head and cocked it at a rakish angle. "You are quite safe with this man." Owela and Elias exchanged looks of understanding.

"I thank you, Elias," Mack said quietly. "Please tell John to come quickly."

"I shall, Miss Mack. All will be well." Then he focused a sober look on Owela. "But I do advise that you take great care, my good fellow." Elias hoisted his pack over his shoulder and gripped his musket. "Ben Sparks is very determined. I think he may not trouble you, but watch your back."

"I know his sort," Owela answered shortly. "I will deal with him properly if he tries to get anywhere near these two."

Elias turned again to Mack and Jamie, his blue eyes twinkling. "We will meet again in time, my young friends. I do want to see that you have both fared well on this adventure. Take note of what Owela tells you and you shall be fine."

"We shall, Elias." Jamie shook Elias' outstretched hand.

"Fare thee well and thank you, Elias," Mack said. He took her hand and lifted it to his lips. "You are a kind man, sir." Mack added. Inwardly, she seethed with anger that they were being left in the charge of this person. Take note of Owela indeed!

So for the next few days they walked back east through the wilderness. The rugged land was heavily wooded and the old trees rose above them. They followed the trade route that ran along the Mohawk River, but stayed away from the path most would have used. There was no need to come upon anyone who might give them trouble, Owela said. He led them around Albany late one night. Irritated that they would not stop even here, Mack could see the faint light glowing from windows as they followed Owela. By the time they stopped hours later, she was furious and would not even look at him as they set up camp.

He was constantly on guard, occasionally stopping to listen for the sounds of footsteps or jingling harnesses. His head tilted to one side, his breath coming slowly and evenly, he would nod once to himself and then motion them on. He did not insist upon silence; he and Jamie got on well and talked quietly as they walked along; now and again they briefly studied the tracks of the animals they saw. Jamie could make the young Oneida's mouth curl in a smile with his nonsense and jokes.

It was not the same thing with Mack. She and Owela had little or nothing to say to each other, it seemed. They tiptoed around each other as though they were lit powder kegs.

"I had not thought to ask you," said Jamie one afternoon as they hiked along a heavily wooded bluff. The leaves were deep here and made a swooshing sound as they walked through them.

"Ask me what, boy?" Owela answered. Mack snorted softly. Boy. He was not so many years older than either of them, and yet he talked as though he was.

"How did you know where to look for us?" Jamie looked at Owela who was walking alongside him, his eyes scanning the forest.

"Yes, do tell us," Mack said, suddenly curious herself. "How did you know where we were?"

Owela looked at Mack. What trap was she setting for him now? Nothing he did seemed to please her, although pleasing her was the last thing on his mind. She did not drop her eyes or look at him carefully from under her lashes like the young women from his village did. This one stared straight at him and asked her question, a slight note of challenge at the edge of her voice. He sighed. "The stones," he explained.

Mack started slightly in surprise but before she could

say anything, Jamie exclaimed, "I thought as much. I knew the sheepshead stones would work, Mack!"

"It was clever of you to drop them on the trail, Jamie," said Owela. "I might not have found the pair of you so easily elsewise, and I am an able tracker."

How like him to brag, thought Mack, but she grudgingly noted that there was no gloating expression on his face. He had simply stated a truth, the same way he might describe the color of his hair or his age.

"Oh, no," Jamie corrected with a shake of his head. "You are wrong. I did not drop the sheepshead stones."

Owela looked at Jamie, confused. Then he let his glance shift to Mack. There was a slight flush on her cheeks. "My pardon," said Owela quietly. "It is you who are the clever one, then."

Mack held herself still for a heartbeat. Of course, he had thought the stones were Jamie's idea and not hers. But then she nodded.

"She said she had a dream about it," offered Jamie.

Owela looked back at Mack, a new light in his eyes. A dream was it? Among his people, dreams were special things. You might find the path your life would take within a dream. Did the English think so as well? But he did not ask. The power of the dream was hers, and if she chose to share it with him, the choice would be hers as well.

Mack, though, said nothing of it, and the moment was lost. She could not tell this young man that John's voice had spoken to her in a dream. She had not even told Jamie. Somehow the dream seemed far too personal to share with anyone. "John told me once that the stones were lucky," she said instead. "I simply hoped that someone would find them."

Owela stopped walking. He fished about in the deerskin bag that hung on a thong around his neck. He held open his palm. In it lay the little sheepshead stones. He dropped them one by one into Mack's open hand.

"They have brought you luck, it seems," said Owela. "You must keep them. Perhaps we shall need that luck yet again." The stones in Mack's hand felt warm and smooth. She pulled open her pouch and quickly put them in.

They walked for a while in silence. Only the calls of blue jays and the swishing of their feet through the leaves could be heard. Locked deep within her thoughts, Mack did not see the strangers who walked through the woods far below the bluff until it was nearly too late.

Owela swore a soft oath under his breath. He had still been thinking about the stones, and he had not been watching as carefully as he usually did. He stepped in front of Jamie and stopped him cold, then, reaching out his hand, grasped Mack's arm and pulled her to a stop. Owela felt her muscles tense and she began to pull away from him. He knew at any moment she would shout her protests aloud as she stiffened herself against the indignity of his unwanted touch.

"Say nothing," he said, pulling her close to him and whispering into her ear, "and take not a step. You must be very quiet or it may cost you your life." A single twig cracking beneath their moccasins might give them away.

Mack looked down. Below them, half-hidden by

bushes and the low sweep of bare branches, a party of men crunched through the fallen leaves. She felt the blood leave her face and then, in a hot rush of anger, the color flooded back as she saw the man she detested.

"It is Ben Sparks," mouthed Jamie silently. Mack nodded slightly, almost afraid to breathe or blink her eyes.

Sparks and one of his men wallowed through the forest, pulling a boy along with them. He will be sold, thought Mack. A pang of pity clutched her heart. Does his mama know what has happened to him? She turned her face and spoke softly into Owela's ear. "Is there nothing we can do? They will sell that child. They have surely stolen him as they took us."

Owela's hand still held her arm. He let it drop suddenly. "Only if you would chance being taken again yourselves," he whispered, and so they watched the party move away. Just before they disappeared into the distance, Ben Sparks' voice rose in the still air. Mack felt the hairs on her neck and arms rise as the cruel, careless words drifted to her ears.

"Step briskly, I say, before a mood comes upon me. We've a long ways to go before we stop for the night." Then the group passed on and the shapes of men faded into the brush.

Owela pulled them both to the ground. He motioned that they should be still. Mack's heart was beating so hard that she was certain Ben Sparks would hear it and come straight to where she crouched, her hands pressed on the damp ground. Many minutes passed, and then Mack felt Owela's warm breath again as he leaned close and spoke quietly.

"We will go back," he said. "An hour ago there was a place where we may pass the night hidden from anyone who comes by."

They stood and turned their backs on the woods below them. Owela led them slowly, carefully down the bluff in the opposite direction from Sparks and his group. On this side of the rise, rocky ledges and walls jutted out from between the trees and bushes. They picked their way gingerly down and then followed a shallow stream that flowed at the bottom for a mile or so. Owela scanned the hill that rose above them. Then he stopped.

"Up there is a safe place," he said quietly. He began to walk.

Mack and Jamie followed him through the thick brush. Branches caught at Mack's hair and scratched her face and arms. Owela pushed back a clump of rhododendron that hung in their path and there it was — a dark opening in the rocky wall. It was a cave. Owela stooped and entered; Jamie and Mack did the same. They stopped only a few feet beyond the entrance.

"How did you know this was here?" Jamie asked in wonder. He looked around. The cave was very dark where it stretched out beyond them.

"I have traveled these places all my life," answered Owela while he checked his musket. "I once stayed in this cave for three days and nights. It was a sudden winter storm that stopped me." Owela set his face and looked directly at Jamie and then Mack. There was no compromise in his dark eyes. "You will stay here and not leave this cave for any reason. Do you hear me? It does not matter why you think you must, you will stay here and be silent. I will go back and track them. I must be certain they have not seen us and are even now following." They watched Owela leave the cave's low entrance. The bushes snapped back into place, hiding the opening once again.

It was several hours before Owela returned. Mack and Jamie had sat close by the cave's opening. Neither wished to venture farther back into the blackness. They wrapped the blankets around themselves and sat huddled together against the cold and dampness. Mack watched the late sky change from softly clouded blue, to pink, and then deepen to a velvety dark sweep. A full moon rose. There was the slightest rustle — it might have been the wind — and then Owela pulled back the bush and stooped to enter the cave.

"They are far gone from here," he told them. "They are moving very quickly and did seem keen to get to their destination, wherever that may be." Mack remembered their days with Ben Sparks and she fought the urge to shudder. She did so anyway and her teeth began to chatter.

"Might we at least have a fire?" Jamie asked in a tired voice. "Is it safe for us to make a fire and warm ourselves? Mack will not admit it, but I shall. I truly believe my bottom is half-frozen."

"Yes," Owela answered kindly, chuckling softly. "But we shall move far back into the cave for that." He took

Jamie's arm, and Jamie, in turn, clasped Mack's hand. Then slowly, slowly, they moved into the hill.

CHAPTER SEVEN

Mack could not tell how far back into the cave they went, for in the darkness she had no sense of direction at all. She felt somehow that other people had been there before. The path was clear and dry and there were no stones over which she might have stumbled. When they stopped, she was surprised to see a milky patch of light on the floor. She looked up. There was the moon, clearly visible through a hole in the cave's ceiling.

Owela looked up himself. "You would not believe it, but the snow and rain cannot really get in."

"What an odd place this is," Jamie exclaimed with interest. He peered around curiously and looked back toward the darkness. The cave was large, stretching back a number of feet and opening to a higher ceiling that disappeared into blackness.

"Look just beyond where the cave widens. Perhaps there is still a bit of wood there for a fire," Owela said to Jamie.

Jamie groped his way back along the wall; just enough moonlight lit the shadows for him to see more or less where he was going. In the shadowy darkness he found a dry pile of wood, small branches and heavier windfall logs of beech and red oak. He returned with a bundle of sticks and small logs in his arms.

Owela struck flint and steel together. When smoke rose from the tinder, he carefully nursed a small fire into a warming blaze, while Jamie and Mack piled their gear out of the way against the cave's walls.

"There is water here, as well," Owela said as he fanned the flames. "A small underground stream. It pools just over there. Can you see it?"

"We will have a fire and water, but there is no food," Jamie grumped. He shrugged his shoulders. "Well, there is nothing to do about that, I suppose."

"There is food, though you may not care for it," Owela answered. He opened his hunting pouch. "I have parched corn and venison jerky with me always. We have not needed it until now. We will hunt tomorrow, Jamie, but this must do until then."

"Will it be wise to hunt?" Jamie asked, taking a handful of corn from Owela and passing it to Mack. "Will it be safe to fire your musket?"

"With bow and arrow, safe enough," said Owela. He would not risk the far-reaching sound of musket fire in the forest's still air. Better to go hungry than to bring Ben Sparks upon them.

"It is hard to chew." Jamie grimaced as he ate the small portion Owela gave him.

"But it is good," Mack admitted. Then quietly she said to Owela, "I thank you."

Her stomach still felt hollow. A bit of meat and corn had not been enough for her, but she never would have said a word or asked for more. Mack could not understand Owela at all. He did not seem to feel the cold or ever tire on the trail. Not a single time in this last week had she heard his stomach rumble. More than once her own had betrayed her, unearthly sounds rising from the depths to announce her appetite.

"You are welcome, Mack," Owela told her. "I am happy to share with you." For some reason she felt herself color.

"You know this cave, you said," she blurted out, to turn the talk and her thoughts from her belly and food. Owela sat there near the fire, lit by the red light of the coals. His legs were crossed and his elbows rested on his knees. There was a tension in his face and he was thinner than when she had first seen him. He is as tired and hungry as I am, thought Mack with a slight shock, and she felt guilt nag at her a bit.

"Yes," he answered her. "I spent three days here once, and it was far colder than this. How the snow blew! The wind howled like a wolf down through that hole above us." Owela's eyes lit suddenly, and the weariness fell from him like a soft cloak dropping to the ground. He stood and thrust a dry branch into the fire. When its end blazed, he pulled it out and held the torch above his head.

"What is it?" asked Jamie. "What are you doing?"

"Well, come along and see," Owela said mysteriously. Jamie stood up, his knee joints popping. Mack stood as well.

"Lead on," she said lightly.

As they walked back into the cave, the ceiling opened. The walls widened and great patches of smooth rock shone dully in the wavering light of the burning stick. There was the occasional drip of water but, except for that, the air was quiet and very close. Owela paused and held up his hand.

"A moment," he said softly as he held the torch higher. "I am certain it is near. It cannot have flown away into the sky."

Mack drew in her breath. On the rock wall were lines of faint blue and rusty red. In the poor light she could not make out their shape or tell what it was. Suddenly, it all fell into place. There was a wide sweep of curving wing and the graceful arch of a slender body. She reached out her hand and brushed the painted stone with her fingertips. "It is a dragonfly," she whispered in delight. She leaned toward the image.

"Yes," said Owela, holding the torch closer. "But there is something else. You must go very quietly for I would not have them waken. I think they may still be here. It is the time for them, after all," Owela said thoughtfully.

Mack blinked in surprise. "Who? Does someone live in this cave? Or something?" She looked uneasily back over her shoulder, but the thick darkness showed her nothing.

Mack felt the hairs on the back of her arms begin to prickle and rise as goose bumps crept across her skin. She could hear Jamie breathing beside her. There was a tension in the still air. It was the same tension she had sensed once or twice the past summer in a storm on the water, seconds before a bolt of lighting split the sky. When Owela stopped, she nearly bumped into him, so closely had she been following.

"Look up," he said in a voice that was barely a whisper, and their eyes lifted to the roof of the cave. At first it seemed to Mack that the stony arch curving above her was covered with brown moss. She squinted her eyes and looked again, then turned to Owela, opening her mouth to speak. He motioned her to silence.

Hundreds of bats hung upside down, the claws of their tiny feet clutching the rocky crevices. Wrapped in their delicate wings, the bats crowded shoulder to shoulder, a living carpet. They were as still as though they were carved of stone. Then one of the creatures stretched and yawned, its teeth shining in the torch's light like tiny ivory needles. Owela made a slight motion with his hand, and they carefully crept back to their campsite. He tossed the torch into the flames as they all dropped down around the fire's warmth.

"In the summer evenings, the bats will fly out that opening atop the cave," he told them, gesturing to the hole. "They sleep here all winter upside down, as you saw."

"People say they will tangle themselves in your hair," said Jamie. He looked back to where the bats slept peacefully and set his hands protectively over his head.

Owela laughed softly. "I cannot say one way or the other, although I have not had bats in my own hair. I have seen birds fly into trees or the sides of lodges when the sun is in their eyes, and yet I have never seen a bat do such a thing, even in the night."

Jamie sat quietly. Best not to wake the bats, no matter how well they might fly. "That dragonfly," he asked in a whisper. "What is it? How did it ever get here?" He waited for Owela to answer him, but Owela just sat quietly, staring into the low flames.

"It would be a painting set upon the stone by a young boy," he said at last.

Jamie stared at him in confusion. "How can you tell that?" he asked.

Owela leaned back on his elbows and looked up through the hole in the cave's ceiling where now only the edge of the round moon could be seen. How might he explain such a thing to Jamie? "When a boy comes to a certain age, he goes off by himself with only his weapons," Owela began in a low voice. "He does not know where he will go or where his journey will take him. It is all part of the dream he seeks."

"Did you ever do such a thing?" asked Mack.

Owela raised his eyebrows in amazement that she was even interested in the painting or anything he might have done. She looked away, then looked back at him, waiting for what he would say. He sat up and crossed his legs.

"Yes, I did," he answered, "but I would not talk of it, nor my dream. It is something you do not share with just anyone." To his wonder, she nodded. Then he remembered — she had had her own dream weeks ago while he searched for them, and she had not shared it, either.

Perhaps she understood more than he thought.

"Fair enough," agreed Mack. "But why the painting? Why would a boy paint a dragonfly on the wall of a cave?"

Owela looked at her thoughtfully. She had laid no traps for him these last days. There had been no arguments since he had given her back the sheepshead stones, although she had made it clear she did not wish to travel in his company. Still, there was always a small current of something that ran between them, like the unseen tug of a powerful river when you waded out past the shallows. One slip and you would be gone.

"He would have slept here and waited for his dream. It would have been cold in this place, but he must have been a clever lad. The wood and tinder at the back of the cave must have been brought in by him. He might have fasted. Some do. Water alone would have kept him alive. When he slept and the dream came, he painted what he saw."

"He dreamed of a dragonfly, then?" said Mack, and for an instant she saw the *Odonata* in her mind's eye, skimming across the ocean, its sails billowing in the strong wind. She felt a pang of loneliness for John and their happy life with him.

"He did," answered Owela as he tossed wood chips into the fire. "He would have ground red and blue stones to make the colors. Perhaps he used the blood of an animal he hunted or a bit of fat to set the paint. And when the painting was finished, the dragonfly would be his symbol for all time."

"What if he had dreamed of a skunk?" teased Jamie, and although Owela's mouth twitched at such silliness, his eyes remained serious.

"Then it would have been the skunk that became his symbol. It does not matter what thing or animal a boy dreams of. They all have their place. They all have their own meaning." A hidden nugget of sap in the firewood made a small pop as he went on. "The dragonfly is quick and free like a whirlwind. It will not be still for long."

Owela wondered if either of them would ask about what he had dreamed. But they both sat quietly. Unable to keep his eyes open, Jamie yawned and put his head down on his raised knees. The silence was as thick as the darkness. Suddenly, there was a dreadful sound. Owela felt the blood rise up his neck, as Mack stared at him.

"Well, well," she said archly, but then she smiled. "I do believe from the sounds your stomach is making that you are as hungry as I must admit I am. You say that you and Jamie may hunt tomorrow along the way?"

"We will hunt," Owela answered, grateful for the words that would mask the sound of his complaining belly. "There will be fresh meat tomorrow, fear not."

"Well, until then, I hope your stomach does not call Ben Sparks back here," she joked, but then the smile left her face. It was not anything to joke about at all.

"He will not come back here, and, if he does, I will deal with him," Owela replied. "And you have the pistol. You know how to use it well, I seem to recall, although I do not think you would have."

She opened her mouth to say something in her own

defense, but he pointed with his chin at Jamie, who was asleep, his forehead resting on his knees, little snores coming from him. Mack met Owela's eyes and, for the first time since they had been together, they smiled shyly at each other. She covered Jamie with the blanket they shared. Jamie started, looked around himself, and then lay down. "Come to bed," he muttered sleepily.

"It is still a hard journey," Owela said. He tossed a small log on the flames, pulled a blanket over his shoulders, and sprawled out by the fire. "The land is hilly, but we can be in Boston in a few days if we push hard." He studied Jamie. "He does well, but he is not a strong lad, is he?"

"Strong enough," Mack insisted. "Jamie manages. He is tired, but he would never give up."

That must be a trait common to all MacNeils, Owela thought to himself, but he only said, "We will go as quickly as we are able, but we must not wear ourselves down."

"Good enough," whispered Mack. "This has been dreadful. I have been cold and filthy for days and days, and yet a part of me does not want it to end." She eased Jamie over on his side, and he grumbled a bit as he wriggled to make himself comfortable.

Owela propped himself up on his elbow. "What do you mean? It seems to me that you have hated every moment of this. When it is done, you may return to England. Your home is there, is it not?"

Very well, Mack thought. He has asked and I shall tell him. "When it is over we shall surely return to England.

Do you actually think I long for that place? Oh, I know I have not wanted to go with you to Boston, but that is only because it meant I would be that much closer to leaving Canada. It was nothing personal, you must know. I am not certain where my home is any longer. I only know that since I have been here, I have been happy. Jamie has as well." She ran her hands through her hair and shook her head. "I have been rude and thoughtless and unpleasant to you, but there was no one else upon whom I might have taken out my anger. Ben Sparks, perhaps, if I could have set my hands on him." She stared hard at Owela.

"I see."

"What do you see?"

Owela lay down again, cradling his head on his arm. "I see you sitting there and you are most angry. Perhaps tomorrow will be different. Who can say how things may change?"

"A feather bed will be a welcome change from this," Mack admitted. She shifted around on the cold ground under the blanket next to Jamie. It was hopeless. This night would be as uncomfortable as all the others. She heaved a tired sigh as she tried to put an end to the day. After a while, Mack fell asleep, and, thankfully, did not dream at all. And Owela was left awake to wonder what it might be like to sleep in a bed of feathers like some strange bird.

CHAPTER EIGHT

They arrived in Boston on a cloudy afternoon in early December. In spite of the fading light, many people were still out and about. Wagons and carts moved up and down the city's streets, their wheels making low, creaking rumbles.

There were churches everywhere. Slender steeples poked into the sky and bells rang out in the damp air. Houses crowded against each other. Through the windows, Owela could see many candles burning. How strange it was that these people must have their lodges lit as though with the sun. He glanced at Mack. Was this the life she knew and in time would return to?

"Boston. It seems odd to be here again." Mack let her eyes move over the houses and people. She had not cared much for the weeks spent in the forests, the roughly cooked meals and nightly beds on one hard patch of ground or another. Yet seeing the city and all these people only reminded her of England. The bittersweet image of Brierly, forgotten for a short while, rose up in her mind like a ghost. She shivered and then shook her head slightly. She would not think about it or let anything haunt her.

Jamie lifted his shoulders in a gesture of confusion. "Where shall we go?"

"Let us make our way to the harbor, Jamie. *Odonata* will be there somewhere," Mack answered. She looked around herself and then began to walk in the first direction that seemed right.

"No," Owela said shortly. He stepped in front of her, ready for the argument he was absolutely certain would come. "You have no idea where you are going. Neither do I. We must find this man, this friend of John's. Paul Revere, he is called. John said he is a silversmith. He will give us directions and tell us about what hazards may wait for us here."

"Listen to me, if you please," Mack stormed. "We are tired and dirty and half-starved. You have led us across the entire countryside over some of the worst land I have ever seen. Hills, you called them! They were mountains in my opinion, and not once would you stop near any place remotely civilized." She rubbed the back of her grimy hand across her forehead, leaving a smear of dirt. "Surely, Paul Revere may wait for just an hour while we go to the ship. I must bathe. I can bear this no longer!"

Owela said nothing at all. He simply stared at Mack, his face expressionless. There was a long silence as they stood there in the street, with Jamie shifting from one foot to another. Finally she threw her hands up into the air.

"Very well, then," she huffed. "It will be your way, if it must, and I see that it must. Lead on to Paul Revere, wherever in Boston he may be."

"A silversmith, is he? Then he must have a shop," said Jamie in relief. There would be no squabbling for the moment. "That should be easy enough. I will ask this woman the way."

A carriage waited in the street for the woman who was just getting in, her silk skirts lifted so that they might not be soiled. Mack pushed the loose strands of her uncombed hair off her face as she and Owela followed Jamie. She saw the woman's eyes widen when Jamie stopped at the carriage. He leaned toward the window to speak to her, a smile on his face, and placed his hand upon the carriage door.

"Enough of that! Get your filthy hand off this carriage and step away before I take my whip to you," warned the coachman harshly. "Away I tell you!"

Jamie stepped back and put both hands behind his back, lest his knuckles get smacked. His face flamed. "I only wished to ask for directions, sir," he tried to explain. "We need help finding our way, and I thought perhaps you might be of assistance. I meant no harm."

The woman rapped on the roof of the carriage. "Drive on. I cannot bear the sight of these beggars, much less the dreadful smell!" she whined in a bored tone. "It is a disgrace how many ruffians wander the streets of Boston these days shouting one slogan or another."

"Liberty, indeed," the coachman rumbled, clenching the reins. Then his voice rose. "If liberty means that such trash as you might feel free to approach and speak to a fine woman like my mistress, may our ties with England never be broken."

"You are rude!" cried Mack hotly. "We are no more beggars than you are. We simply seek the way to the shop of Paul Revere, the silversmith."

"Really?" drawled the woman, looking Mack up and down and casting a doubtful eye on Jamie and Owela. "For what? Murder? Robbery? You two dirty boys and the creature who accompanies you certainly mean no good." She pressed a scented lace handkerchief to her nose and tapped again upon the inside of the carriage roof.

"Move away or have your toes ground to mush!" threatened the coachman in a low growl. He snapped the reins over the horses' backs. The carriage began to roll. "And be well gone from here or I shall call the soldiers and have you taken away!" he cried over his shoulder.

Mack and Jamie stood in stunned silence, their mouths open. Unlike them, Owela was not surprised. It was not the first time in his life he had been treated this way, spoken to as though he was of little or no worth. Such things did not happen among his own people. There he was treated with respect. Outside the ordered world of the longhouse, things could be different. He had seen the looks cast his way by traders and soldiers, and he knew very well what they were thinking.

"Dirty boys," raged Mack. She made a rude noise and furiously brushed her hair back from her face. "How dare that pampered fool speak to us in such a manner. This is worse than England could ever be!"

"What about the creature?" asked Jamie in a small

voice. "We must not forget the creature." He looked at Owela who, to his surprise, had a mischievous glint in his eyes.

"Why should I be the one to take offense? You make your judgments hastily," said Owela. "I think that woman did not speak of me at all."

"Whatever do you mean?" Mack snapped her head around to stare at him. "Have you not the sense to be offended?" Owela leaned on his musket and looked Mack up and down with the same disdain the woman had. Oh, no! thought Jamie. Now we are in for it.

"Well," Owela said slowly. "It seems to me that I am a man, and young Jamie here, he is a boy. Dirty as we are, it is easy enough for anyone to see. Now I ask myself, who and what does that leave?"

Jamie dared not look at Mack, who now stood with her hands on her hips and bright color on her smudged cheeks.

"Do you mean to say that woman was calling me a creature? Is that what you are saying?" she cried. With her tangled hair and the sparks that flew from her blue eyes, she did seem like some sort of wild thing.

She took a step forward to tear into Owela, when suddenly she heard a high giggling. A small boy of perhaps six years was watching them from where he stood near one of the shops. The child's face was dirty and his eyes were like dark, shiny pebbles. He wore shabby, worn clothing and his ruined shoes were wrapped with rags. Blonde hair flopped over his brow. The boy smiled widely as his eyes danced over each of them in turn.

"Are you laughing at me as well?" asked Mack. This was too much to bear.

The little boy giggled again. "Yes, miss, but I cannot help it," he answered, struggling with his laughter. "You do look so funny right now. Almost as though you are going to explode!"

"I just may explode. I certainly am cross enough to do so!" Mack grumbled hopelessly. She looked sideways at Jamie, who was battling to keep his face straight. Owela she pointedly ignored for the moment. "See here, child, might you help us?"

"Oh, yes, miss! Do you need food and drink? I know a tavern where they throw very tasty scraps out into the alley. If you know when they empty the cook pots, you can usually get them before the rats do. But you have to be fast! And you could wash your faces and hands — not that they are really in need of it. Only a little perhaps," he offered hesitantly. Mack did not know whether to laugh or cry. Poor thing, poor little boy, to live in such a way.

"I am filthy," she said gently, "and so are these other two *creatures*. I would dearly love a good meal, although I doubt I could be faster than the rats. It seems that nothing at all shall happen though, until we first find the shop of Paul Revere. Might you know the way?" She crouched down next to the boy and took his small hands in hers. He glowed with pleasure at her touch.

"Everybody knows that shop," the boy answered eagerly. "I can take you there."

Thomas was the child's name. Thomas and nothing

more. He talked steadily as he took them down the street.

Many of the shops were still open, although afternoon had turned to early evening. Buttery light spilled out from the glass panes onto the street. Signs hung above some of the doorways, announcing their wares. From copper to fabrics, from carefully crafted furnishings to spices and tea, each shop carried something different. Servants bustled in and out, carrying packages for their employers. Carriages and horses waited in the street. The air was pungent with the scent of animal sweat and droppings.

The smell was overpowering. Scents of people and horses were mixed with the odors of rotting food and the contents of chamber pots that were now and again tossed out of open windows. After weeks in the forests, with their clear, fresh air, they all found themselves breathing through their mouths.

"My word, but the stench of this place is strong," Jamie said, making gasping noises and grasping at his throat in high drama. Owela seemed to find this very amusing, and even Mack, as irritated as she was with all that had happened so far in Boston, could not keep from smiling a little.

"That is what everyone says when they come here," said Thomas, carefully sidestepping a steamy pile of dung. "Although I hardly notice it myself, sir. The closer you go to the harbor, the more of Boston you smell."

"It is only that we have not been in a city for a long while," Mack explained.

"It needs a good rain to wash away the stink," suggested

Owela, who was watching the cobbles carefully as he walked. "It smells like rain, so we might be in luck."

"How can you smell rain above all this?" laughed Jamie, but Owela only shrugged his shoulders.

"It is here, miss!" cried Thomas. "This is the one." Then, running ahead a little, he stopped in front of a shop and gestured to the door.

"Our thanks, Thomas," whispered Mack. She squeezed his cold hand. "I would give you a coin for your trouble, but I have none. Wait here for us, please, Thomas."

"Oh, that is fine, miss," he assured her. "I do not mind."

Mack pulled open the door and they entered the shop. Jamie and Owela moved forward, but Mack looked back and saw Thomas standing alone in the street. How small he seemed. Then the door shut and hid him from her sight.

CHAPTER NINE

Inside the shop, a stout, cheerful-looking man turned his attention to them. There were several display tables between him and them. The polished surfaces were covered with mugs and cutlery, plates and bowls, and tea services.

"Good evening, sirs!" said the man warmly. Then he squinted his eyes and blinked a few times. In front of him waited three travel-stained people. What he had at first mistaken for a tall, young man was clearly a young woman. The loose breeches and baggy shirt hid any feminine charms she might possess. Her face was strong and serious. Two young fellows stood nearby, almost hovering over her. One, the boy, must certainly be a relative. The other, a Native, held his face carefully blank as he watched Revere. Both young men were poised to protect the young lady if any move were made against her.

"I ask your pardon, miss. It was the light, I do believe. How might I help you, miss?" he asked gently.

"You are thoughtful to say so. I know I look a sight."

Mack walked toward him, navigating between the silver-covered tables, followed by Jamie and Owela. "I think you can, sir. At least, I hope you will be so kind as to do so."

Just before she reached him, her hip brushed a small table and it tottered upon its thin legs. The tall coffee pot that stood on its surface tilted and then fell. Owela thrust out a hand and caught it. As he did, the silver locket that had hung around his neck all this time slipped out from under his shirt. Owela straightened up and handed the pot carefully to Revere.

"My thanks, sir. You are quick," Revere said to Owela. He pointed to the locket. "May I?" Then he reached out and picked up the silver ornament, turning it this way and that so that the candle's light shone on its carved and shining cover.

"It is beautiful, is it not?" piped up Jamie.

"It is that, I must admit," Revere laughed. "Although I do dislike boastfulness in a man." And he chuckled again to see their puzzled stares. "You see, I made this locket myself."

"Of course," said Mack slowly, as it all became clear to her. "That is how John knows of you, Mr. Revere."

Paul Revere smiled at their astonished faces. Then he turned his full attention to Owela. "But what I wonder is, how do you come to be wearing the locket, sir?" he asked with friendly curiosity in his voice.

Revere had immediately recognized his own fine work. It was a perfectly shaped oval of silver. On the polished lid were the raised apple blossoms that John

MacNeil had requested he create. On the back was a set of initials — CM — carefully and ornately engraved; his own maker's mark was below them. He dropped the locket back down onto Owela's shirt.

"My friend John MacNeil gave it to me," answered Owela, looking back at Revere levelly. "He would never have done so if he did not trust me with so precious a thing."

"I do recall that John told me he meant to paint a miniature of his ward and place it within." Revere's tone was thoughtful.

"See it for yourself," said Owela. He popped open the locket and held it so that Revere could see inside. There was the tiny painting, a rather tidier version of the girl who stood in front of him.

Revere peered at the image, then he turned to Mack. "Are you Lord MacNeil's ward? What on earth has happened here, child?"

"Yes, I am," said Mack, and she told him the story of what had passed these last weeks. She spoke slowly and quietly, and, as she did so, the fear and desperation that she had felt when they were in the hands of Ben Sparks came creeping back.

"You are brave, indeed," said Revere when she finished, but she shook her head.

"I am not brave at all," Mack answered. She felt drained. "You do what you must. Besides, there were friends who helped us." Her eyes moved once to Owela, who lifted his brows at her words. He said nothing, though, and only stood near her, quietly listening and watching.

"Well," Revere mused, "it is late, but if you must go to the ship, then I shall escort you all. I have seen *Odonata* tied there just this day. It is lucky that she is at one of the wharves rather than out at anchor. What a fuss it would be to call for a launch and go out onto the harbor at this hour. I will lock up here and then we shall be off."

Outside the shop, Mack looked around for the little boy who had helped them, but Thomas was gone and the street was still and silent. How sad, she thought as they followed Revere. The child had seemed small and so very alone. Then she thought of what Molly Ladle had said about helping someone in need. Molly helped us. It would have been so easy to do something for the poor little boy, Mack told herself. I should have insisted that Thomas wait. He might have come with us to the ship. She hoped he had a warm place to sleep and was not even now wandering the city.

They hurried down Boston's dark, chilly streets to the waterfront. Mack could see the lights of ships out on the water. They reached the wharf and started out along it. There were other vessels tied there, but Mack knew *Odonata* at once when she saw her.

"There she is!" cried Jamie. "I do not think she has changed at all since we last were on her here in Boston. My word, she does look quite wonderful, does she not, Mack?"

"Yes," said Mack. "She is a fine sight, Jamie!"

In spite of the fact that the ship would in time carry her back to England, it did look wonderful to Mack's eyes. The carved figurehead of a woman still looked out from beneath the long sprit at the bow. The huge sails were neatly furled upon the yards, the watch stood quiet and sharp-eyed on the deck, and the sound of a fiddle rose into the still air from below decks. England's flag, lit by a lantern, lifted and fell in the slight breeze.

"Ahoy, *Odonata*! It is me. Jamie MacNeil," shouted Jamie loudly through cupped hands. "Permission to come aboard?"

Owela looked doubtfully at him. "You ask permission to go onto your own ship?"

"Oh, it is the MacNeil ship and so ours as well, but we always do this," Jamie laughed. "It is most nautical, you see."

"If that is young Master Jamie, then he may indeed come aboard," a voice called back. Jamie ran ahead, up the gangplank and onto the ship. Mack could hear the thudding of his feet on the deck and the sound of his excited voice as he shouted to the sailors.

"Will you come aboard, sir?" she asked happily, turning to Paul Revere who stood near her. "May I repay your kindness with hospitality? You might take a glass of port and warm yourself."

"No, I shall not, Miss MacNeil, although it is a great temptation," Revere answered, bowing over her hand. "You will be comfortable and secure here tonight, and you have had quite enough excitement for a while. I must be off to my home and my family. I will look for word of you each day, though. Come to my shop now and again so that I may see that you are doing well. And you must let me know if you want for a single thing. John

MacNeil would not thank me for letting harm come to any of you."

"Harm? What harm can come to us here?" Mack asked him, her eyes wide. "Surely we are in no danger aboard this armed ship."

Revere gave Owela a meaningful glance. He could see by the set of the fellow's jaw and the way he stood close by the girl that the young man knew very well such a city was filled with dangers.

"Boston is considered to be rather a bomb at the moment, miss. The fuse of that bomb has not yet been lit, but it shall be. Of that I am as certain as I am that there will be a war of revolution in time. That alone should be enough to keep you on board this vessel. And do not give me that look, Miss MacNeil. Oh, I have no doubt you will go wandering the city, but if you think that the clothing you wear will shield you, you are mistaken. At the very least, keep this fine fellow by your side as protection."

"She knows that," Owela said, before Mack could answer. "She will not be out of my company for a moment." Mack huffed softly at this. "Can you send word to John?"

"I will do my best. Anyone I know who travels west and may meet him will say that you are safely here. A good night to you both then." Revere bowed to Mack, turned, and made his way down the wharf.

Mack turned her back on Owela and sprinted up the gangplank to where Jamie now stood with the ship's skipper, Captain Apple. They must get below and warm themselves, the captain exclaimed, shaking his head over their sorry condition. Their berths and cabins were ready as always. What in the world were they doing here? And where was Lord MacNeil? Jamie and Mack went down the companionway and walked through the ship to the stern, quickly answering all of his questions. They reached Jamie's cabin and followed him in.

"We are fine, now that we are here on the ship," Mack said to Captain Apple. They dropped their packs to the floor. "We have sent word to Niagara that we are safe. Surely, John will come for us soon."

"I am certain he will, miss," the captain assured her. He grumbled to himself over the thought of what had happened to these two. He quickly lit the charcoal in a small brazier that stood in a corner. The cabin would soon be warm. "I myself shall light the brazier in your cabin as well, miss. Sleep well, Master Jamie." The captain touched a hand to his tricorne and then left them alone.

"Get into your berth, Jamie. You are shivering with the cold. Here. Just slip off your moccasins. No matter how we smell, I do think you might sleep in your clothing one last time. I will find cook and get something hot for you to drink."

"Owela," said Jamie. He lay back and sighed with relief.

"Who? Oh, yes, Owela," Mack said as she fussed around the cabin looking for bedding. "What of him?"

Jamie shivered and pushed his hair from his eyes. "Owela. You remember Owela, do you not? The good fellow who has helped us to get here alive? Where is he?"

Mack stood by the berth, a feather quilt in her arms. She had not cared until then where Owela might be. He had haunted her every moment for so long, always there guarding and giving endless cautions. What a pleasure she had thought it would be to feel free of his presence and orders. Then she felt a hot rush of shame. Those orders had saved their lives.

She flung the quilt over Jamie's head and cleared her throat. "I will find him."

"Yes, do," came the muffled reply.

Mack walked silently back through the ship. The sound of the fiddle had stopped, for it was late. She stepped out into the cold air. The ship was dark except for the lanterns of the sailors on watch, and only the stars and a lopsided moon lit its deck. Owela stood by the rail, looking out over the wharf. He had wrapped a blanket around himself. The wind was up now and his long hair whipped about his shoulders. Hearing her footsteps, he turned.

"What is this?" Mack asked him impatiently. "Surely you cannot think to stay out here? Why did you not come below with us?"

"There is no need to trouble yourself," he answered her, just as impatiently. "I may guard you just as well here as within the ship."

"Guard us? You need not guard us at all anymore," Mack said, her voice rising a little. "Truly. There is not a thing that may harm us here."

"I will not leave you until you are safely in John's hands. I gave my word to him as his friend," Owela insisted. "Have you no understanding of friendship?"

With a resigned sigh, Mack realized she had had enough of arguing with Owela. She crossed her arms over her chest, suddenly very chilly and quite exhausted.

"Very well. Stand guard all night if you will," she told him firmly. "But if you must, do so below, or I will stay out here with you. Why should this night be different from any other? I am almost used to sleeping out in the cold by now."

"Where would you build your fire?" He looked sideways at her, amused that she would say such a thing. She was nearly frozen and was shivering visibly. "You cannot sleep without one, as I clearly recall."

"You are correct. I cannot. There is already one burning in the brazier in my cabin right now. It is quite cozy there, I suspect." Mack took a deep breath and looked away. "I do understand what friendship is about, you know, Owela. I did mean what I said in Mr. Revere's shop. I have not once truly thanked you for how you have helped us. I have seemed ungrateful. Until now I was, I suppose, but I have hated how much I needed your help. Can you see that?"

"I understand it," he said gruffly. "It is always best to stand on your own, to be strong and capable."

"Yes. I must be just that for Jamie's sake, as well as for my own." She looked out across the harbor.

"But there are times when two or three together may do better than one," Owela said in a low voice. "There is no shame in taking the help of a friend when it is offered."

She slid her hands in and out of the pockets of John's coat and let out a puff of breath. It made a small cloud and then disappeared. How hard it was to say these things. "See here, then. Might we begin afresh? It seems we will be together for a while longer, and I think it would be rather more pleasant as friends. The three of us as friends, I mean." Mack looked cautiously at him and held out her hand.

Owela nodded briefly. How she continued to astonish him! He himself would not have been able to ask for her friendship. His pride would not have let him, no matter how badly he might long for it — and yet she could do such a thing.

"Of course. We will be friends. The three of us as friends, then," he agreed, and it was a small but distinct pleasure for him to say the words. Taking the hand she offered, he gave it a smart shake. Mack gently pulled back her hand, turned, and led him across the deck. Owela followed her down the stairs to Jamie's cabin.

"Well, there you both are," Jamie observed dryly. "And smiling at that. How amazing. Are the sailors doing amusing things out on the deck?"

"Be quiet and go to sleep," said Mack. "Why should we not be smiling? We finally have a warm, dry place to spend a night."

"I have not slept in such a place before," Owela confessed to Jamie as he peered into the room's corners. "A frontier cabin once or twice. I think I cannot abide the closeness of it. Perhaps the deck would suit me better after all."

"Just think of this as a cabin of another sort," said Mack, with little hope that he would. "There is a different cabin you may have to yourself if you wish, or Jamie will share his place with you and it will be more cheerful."

"Where will you pass the night?" Owela asked.

"In my own cabin just down the passageway," Mack answered. What an odd question! "And it will be a great luxury to be away from the two of you. You both snore hideously."

"What makes you think you do not?" laughed Jamie as Mack opened the door to leave them. "You are nearly as loud as Elias Stack at times!"

Mack scoffed at this. "That is simply not possible. No one snores like Elias Stack."

"I will sleep on the floor," Owela said to Jamie. "It cannot be much harder than the ground, and I have slept on that many times."

This room looked strange to him. It was so different from a longhouse. There were many things in it that seemed to have no purpose. Pictures hung on the walls and braided rugs lay like neat pools of color on the wide pine floorboards. Instead of a sleeping platform, an odd bed hung from the ceiling. It was piled with thick blankets of blue and white.

"Oh, come now," Jamie replied from where he lay with his hands behind his head. "Are you not even a little curious as to what it is like to sleep in a feather bed?" Owela put out a hand and pushed down on the bedding.

It was as soft as a cloud might be.

"It shall be heaven!" said Mack cheerily, and then she disappeared to the privacy and solitude of her cabin.

In time the ship grew quiet. The seamen on watch stood silently in the darkness. Jamie, Mack, and Owela slept, lulled by the gentle movement of the vessel pulling against the lines that tied it to the wharf.

◇ ◇

On the other side of Boston, a man sat in a noisy tavern and nursed a flagon of beer. The room was clouded with the smoke from many clay pipes. A low fire burned in the hearth. The man rubbed a dirty hand across his thin, unshaven face and smoothed back his greasy hair. It was going to be a long search, and he had decided to do it alone. He had coin in his pocket from a recent, and very profitable, sale and could afford to take the time to carry on the hunt properly. All the way to Boston he had come, for something he could not explain told him this was the place to start. There had not been a single moment on that journey when he had not thought of her. He tipped back the flagon and drained it in a gulp.

"Another!" he shouted above the conversation and laughter of the people in the tavern. A passing barmaid poured the amber liquid into his cup, took his money, and swayed away, all in one smooth motion.

"I do sense that it is nearly over," the man said under his breath. "There will be a very happy ending to this tale."

In these last days he had spoken to the sheriff, as well

as to a good number of British soldiers who were here in the city. A generous promise of coin had been made should any information come to him regarding a certain escaped woman, his much valued bond servant. The written descriptions were posted — a friendly printer had helped him compose just the perfect wording. His darling Mack was here somewhere. Ben Sparks knew it in his soul, and he would find her no matter how long it took.

CHAPTER TEN

In the morning Mack woke to the sound of the ship creaking gently around her. She lay in her berth for a while, letting the sense of normalcy seep into her bones. Then she sat up and pushed back the tumble of her hair. There would be many things to do today.

"Did you pass the night comfortably?" she asked Owela later. She was searching for clean clothing for them in the trunks in the main cabin. Some of John's things were there, and although the breeches and shirt were a bit large, Jamie should fill them out better than he would have a few years ago.

"I did, although it was like sleeping inside some big animal with all the sounds the ship makes," Owela said with a small laugh. He took only a shirt and a soft wool blanket from Mack. With the blanket he would make a new breech cloth. His high leather leggings would do him well enough no matter how stained they might be.

"Now you know why John always says a ship seems almost alive to him," Mack answered. At the thought of John, she felt a deep ache of longing for his presence.

Would he come soon? She hoped so, but until he did she would make the best of things here. "I will sort myself out into something that is more an English female than the creature you both think I resemble," she continued briskly. Owela and Jamie both made rude noises. "Then we shall see what the day brings."

Alone in her cabin, Mack washed with water warmed in the galley. She had been far too tired to bathe after all, last night. She glanced over at the clothing she had taken from John's cabin. Then with her hair dripping and a heavy towel wrapped around herself, she opened the trunk that held her own belongings. She lifted out one of her gowns that lay neatly folded there and considered it for a moment. It was made of heavy silk the color of emeralds. With its scooped neck and tightly fitted sleeves it had been quite fashionable three years ago in England.

This will be far too snug and short now, she thought. I was but twelve years old when I wore those gowns last. And besides, when I return to England, gowns and petticoats will be all I will be able to wear. It will be plumed bonnets and boned corsets and shoes of delicate leather.

At the thought of shoes, she looked over at the moccasins she had kicked off. They were worn and battered, but they had served her well these weeks. That decided it. It would be shirt and breeches for as long as possible. She pulled on the garments and went out onto the deck.

"Ah. The very picture of an English lady." Jamie took

her hand and bowed over it. Then he looked up at her and grinned. "Nothing fit you, did it? We have both grown taller."

"It is to your advantage, but not to mine, I fear. You must put up with this creature for a while longer."

"Let us walk through the city," Jamie suggested. His eyes were bright, and for once, he looked well-rested. Mack hugged him.

"Yes, the day is perfect. There is not a cloud in the sky and the breeze is barely cold," Mack agreed, looking to Owela. He said nothing and she felt the fragile peace of last night totter a little. "It is quite safe, I am certain." Then an idea came to her. "Besides, we might find that little boy, Thomas. The least we can do to repay his help is bring him back to the ship and feed him."

Owela shook his head. "How can you know that this city is safe? Have you forgotten Paul Revere's words?" Then he sighed. He did not wish to argue with her and so, reluctantly, he gave in. A short walk might do them no harm. "Very well then, if you both must walk, we will *all* walk. I am armed and you wear your tomahawk, Jamie. You, Mack, also have a weapon should we meet any trouble." Then he frowned as he looked at her waist. "At least, you did last night." She had left the pistol in the cabin.

"No. I will not wear that beastly thing a minute longer. Let us be off." She wanted nothing to remind her of their kidnapping and the wretched Ben Sparks this fine morning.

They set out into Boston. Even at this early hour the

harbor was busy. Sailors and merchants jostled against each other. Children ran up and down the streets, playing and laughing. Women carrying baskets peered into the shop windows to see what they might purchase. Cats sat under the tables of the fishmongers, hoping for something to drop to the ground, and flocks of pigeons flew overhead, their wings clattering.

"Please do not stand so closely to me!" Mack begged in exasperation, when she turned and walked into Owela for the third time. "I mean no offense, and I do appreciate your concern, but I can scarcely move." Owela ignored her and remained near them both, his eyes flickering over the people who strolled through the streets and market.

"I do not like this crowd at all," he said tensely. "Anyone may come upon us, and we would not see them until it was too late."

"Very well. Hover. But for mercy's sake, give me at least a little room to breathe!" She stalked off angrily to examine a stack of cabbages that someone had piled near the wall of an inn.

"I had no idea she was so interested in cabbages. Did you, Owela?" asked Jamie in an innocent tone, but Owela merely sniffed. "Let us buy them all, Mack," Jamie laughed. "You have coins from the ship, do you not?" Then he paused. "What is wrong? Are you ill? My word, Mack, you are as pale as milk!"

Mack did not answer. She stood perfectly still, staring at the sheet posted on the tavern wall, while the city of Boston bustled all around her. Her face was white. Beads of sweat pearled her upper lip. She ripped the paper from where it had been pasted and held it out to Jamie and Owela.

"Read this," she said faintly, her eyes closed.

RUN **Away a White woman called Mack**

She is between 15 *and* 17 *Years of age, big and healthy with dark Hair and Blue Eyes and is likely Dressed as a Man. As she has been for some time past much in the company of a sickly white boy called* Jamie, *she is probably lurking with him. Whoever will deliver her to me in* Boston, *shall receive* Forty Shillings, *besides all Reasonable Expenses.*

signed Ben Sparks

Jamie gripped Mack's arm for fear that she would faint. He could feel her entire body trembling.

Owela lifted his shoulders. "I cannot read," he said without shame. "What does it say, Jamie?"

Jamie gently took the paper from Mack's cold fingers, but he did not release her arm. "It is a notice about a runaway servant," he said slowly. His eyes grew wide as he read the thing aloud. When he was finished he looked up, his face as white as Mack's. "It is signed Ben Sparks."

Owela's look was bleak. "Back to the ship," he ordered. "Now!" He pushed them both ahead of him, and they moved down the street back to the ship.

Mack walked quickly with her eyes cast down to the street. She was suddenly aware of how many soldiers were strolling everywhere. She was certain that at any moment a hand would reach out to grab her arm and seize the prize. They would take her to the sheriff. Sparks would claim her, pay the generous reward, and then what? Gradually, her terror began to change to anger. I will not live like this, she thought. He cannot do this to me! To us! By the time they reached *Odonata*, her face was flushed and she was in a complete rage.

"I will tell Revere about these papers. I think there is not a thing he may do about them, but I will tell him still," Owela assured her as they crossed the gangplank and went onto the deck. Curious sailors looked up from their chores. One stepped forward nervously and approached Mack.

Pulling his knitted cap from his head, he bowed stiffly from the waist. "Miss MacNeil, miss. We have wee problem, I do fear, miss. I saw it only a moment ago."

A wee problem. I am about to be dragged off and sold into slavery, and we have a wee problem, Mack thought wildly. She felt her control and that careful mask she held up to the world about to slip. "What is it, seaman?" she asked as calmly as she could.

The sailor pointed to a coil of line. "Well, miss," he said uncertainly, "it is that." There inside the coil of line, curled like a small caterpillar, Thomas lay sound asleep. When Mack leaned forward and touched his arm, Thomas's eyes popped wide open and he sat up straight.

"Whatever are you doing here, Thomas?" she asked gently, Ben Sparks gone from her thoughts. Suddenly awakened like this, the boy looked so young and very confused. Then he saw her face and, in a rush, he climbed from the rope coil.

"I followed you last night, miss, and when the men were not looking, I came aboard as I thought I might offer you my services this day," he said all in one breath. "I could not be certain you would want me with you, even though you said to wait."

He had slept there all night in the cold, they learned. He had no home and took shelter in whatever doorway or shed or alley he could find. He would work hard and be no bother. He hardly ate at all, and so it would cost them nothing to keep him. He would do anything, anything at all for them. Had he not already shown them how useful he was? He could do much more, for he was a clever boy.

"Hush, now. Eat every bit of that and be silent," Mack told Thomas, while he wolfed down hot soup in the warmth of the ship's main cabin. "You may stay with us as long as you wish." The image of Molly Ladle and her great kindness came into Mack's mind, and she continued. "I will find something warm for you to wear and new shoes so that you shall not have to go about in those rags." Mack pressed her fingertips to her temples. "It is all too much," she said and she burst into tears.

Thomas choked on his soup. Jamie's mouth dropped open in horror.

Owela hesitated, then reached out and squeezed her shoulder. His sure touch comforted her somehow. "Put Ben Sparks from your mind, Mack. He must pass by me to get to any of you."

"I know, Owela. I know," she wept, furious that she was crying at all. The tears were almost painful. "It is just too much."

"Oh, Mack." Jamie put his arms around her. He was close to tears himself. "Nothing will happen to you while I am here. I may be a sickly boy — how dare he put that into print — but he must pass me as well."

Mack hugged Jamie back. Then she scrubbed her hands over her face. "I am done with him! I will not let that animal make me weep again!"

In the afternoon Owela and Thomas went to the silver shop with the news, and that night Paul Revere came to the ship.

"I think, Miss Mack, you will have nothing to worry about if you are discreet. No one will dare board a British ship to search for you. It is well known here that this is Lord MacNeil's vessel. Captain Apple and I will vouch for you all if there is any trouble with this man. If he comes anywhere near you or this ship, he will be arrested," Paul Revere reassured her. They sat quietly below decks in *Odonata*'s main cabin. The lamps swung slightly as the ship shifted and pulled at her dock lines.

"I tore down every one of the papers that I could find today," Thomas told her proudly.

"You are a dear child, Thomas," Mack praised him, although in her heart she felt only a helpless dread.

Thomas was dressed in his new clothing, old things that Jamie had long since outgrown. The little boy had gone up and down the streets, searching the walls of buildings for the postings. He could not read the papers himself, but he knew they had upset Miss Mack.

"I will look for more of them every day, Miss Mack. You must stay here and he will not guess where you are," Thomas insisted.

Mack could scarcely bear the awful idea that they must stay aboard every moment of the day. It was not the ship itself; she loved *Odonata*. It was the thought that Ben Sparks, in his own way, now held her prisoner. It seemed that life was a net slowly slipping closed around her.

"You spoke of revolution," she said to Revere, suddenly changing subjects. "I can almost see it now for myself. I am more than ready to start a revolution aboard this ship, if John does not come soon!" She rose and paced around the cabin, then stopped and leaned her forehead against the cold glass of the windows at the stern.

"That would be a sight," laughed Revere. "But until then, you need this ship for the protection it gives you; however, we do not really need England at all."

"How could the colonies think to survive without England?" Jamie asked as he watched Mack.

"It is the people who will make this place survive," Revere answered ardently. "We will not bear the taxes any longer. There is a wind blowing and it brings with it a smell of freedom."

"But then there must be a war," Jamie exclaimed. "Is anything worth that?"

Mack thought of her own life. What might she do to keep even a small bit of independence in a world that offered her none? She would fight desperately for it, she knew, and she would fight just as hard to escape Sparks if she had to.

"Perhaps freedom is worth it, Jamie," Owela said in a quiet voice.

"There is always a price to pay for the things you want, my friends," Revere told them. "It will be a high price, though I believe that all of us are willing to meet it. But enough of this grave topic now. If it comes to war, you will be far from here, back with your families." They spoke of war no more that night, but Mack could not forget it.

Still, revolution was in the air. The sailors gossiped about things they heard in the taverns. Owela and Jamie talked of what war would be like when they thought Mack was not listening. She could almost feel something happening around her as she walked the deck of *Odonata* each evening. It might have been her imagination, but there was something there, like a spark leaping from a flint and striker to start a small flame in tinder. The flame was growing and it was being carefully fanned by Revere and the other patriots. It would surely turn into a roaring fire in time.

Nearly a week passed aboard the ship, long and uneventful, and although Mack watched for John, he did not come. They each invented small tasks to keep themselves busy. Owela cleaned his musket and Mack's pistol, and then, with nothing else to do, paced the deck endlessly. Jamie, with little luck, tried to teach Thomas his letters. To make things even more miserable, the December weather turned chillier and cold rain began to fall, so they could not even go out onto the deck in comfort. Everyone became snappish and irritable.

Mack took comfort in Thomas and felt her heart opening to him in affection. She tried to find ways to amuse the boy who, accustomed to wandering everywhere, fretted at the fact that she would not let him leave the ship anymore. So he followed her around like a little puppy, chattering and constantly asking if there was anything he might do to help. He carried pots of hot tea from the galley to her, folded and refolded the clothing in her trunk, and swept the floor of her cabin, although it did not need sweeping. Mack said nothing to him, only let him carry on. She knew how grateful he was to be with her and she promised herself that no matter where they eventually went, Thomas would go with them.

One dreary morning, Mack found Jamie draped across his berth, groaning with boredom, legs dangling over the side. Thomas was there with him, restless and wriggly, playing with a deck of well-used cards. She herself was very cranky.

"A story might help," Jamie suggested. "Might you read aloud for a while?"

"Easily done," Mack answered him. "There are many books here." A story would relieve everyone's boredom. It will give me something else to think about as well, she thought, looking over the books on the cabin's shelf.

A small book caught her eye. She pulled out the slim volume and, slowly turning the pages, smiled as she translated the title in her head, for it was all in French: *Stories or Tales from Times Past, with Morals*. Inside the book, on the title page, were the same words, but beneath them was a subtitle: *Tales of Mother Goose*. It was Perrault's well-known book of stories for children.

"This one will do," she announced. She pulled a chair close to Jamie and read the title aloud. "Cinderella; or, the Little Glass Slipper."

"Yes, I like that one," said Jamie, sitting up in the berth. He flipped his pillow over to its cool side and made himself comfortable. "I have heard it a thousand times," he confessed, "but it is still a good tale. You will enjoy it, Thomas, and you, as well, Owela."

Mack looked over at Owela, who leaned against the doorjamb, his arms crossed at his chest. "I would not think such a thing would be a wise idea. How could you make your way though the forest in slippers of glass?" he asked. Mack and Jamie glanced at each other.

"She does not run through the forest, Owela," explained Jamie. "She lives in a town like, well, very like Boston."

"Poor girl," Owela shook his head in pity. "I could never live in such a place!"

She started to read, translating the French into English as she went along. Neither Thomas nor Owela would have understood the story otherwise. Thomas did not speak French at all. And although Owela used French for trading, the story was written in the pure French of the court. "There was once upon a time, a widower who married for his second wife the most haughty and proud woman that ever was known on the earth. She was a widow and had two daughters of her own vile humor, who were exactly like her in every way. He had himself a young daughter. This dear girl was the picture of goodness and sweetness."

"That man is an idiot," commented Thomas. "Why does he marry such a horrid woman?"

"I have no idea," said Mack helplessly. "To keep his house? Because he loves her?"

"I would not have such a haughty, proud female in my longhouse!" snorted Owela. "Likely, she could not skin a raccoon." Jamie covered his eyes with one hand.

"Hush!" ordered Mack. She read on. "The stepmother forced her to do the hardest work of the house. She had to dust and clean and polish the fine rooms of her stepsisters and stepmother. The poor child herself had only a wretched bed of damp straw."

"My da is my stepfather. He never did such a thing to me nor my mother," scoffed Owela. "And why does the girl stay in this house?"

"Yes," agreed Thomas in disgust. "She may have to sleep on straw — that is no real hardship, and I have slept on worse — but is she so thick to not have dry straw, at least?"

"She is not thick at all," cried Mack. "It is just a story."

"Has this girl a name?" asked Owela. Now Jamie covered his mouth.

"What is wrong, Jamie? Do you feel as though you will be ill?" Thomas asked him. "Should I get a basin for you?"

"Her name is Cinderella," Mack announced loudly.

"What does it mean?" asked Owela in confusion.

Jamie made squeaking noises from behind his hands. Pink color began to rise up Mack's neck.

"It means nothing! They call her that because she is always covered in ashes." Owela rolled his eyes at this foolishness.

"It will be fine," Jamie told him. "Her fairy godmother will come and bring her clean clothing. She will go to the castle and dance with the prince."

"In the glass slippers?" Thomas asked incredulously.

"Enough!" Mack commanded them all. "One more word from any of you and I shall not read this!" She looked at each of them to make certain they understood she meant her threat.

When the cabin was silent, she began to read again. Her voice took on a cadence that was soothing and quiet. Jamie leaned his head back and closed his eyes as he listened with a smile on his face. Thomas curled up next to him. Owela crossed the room to sit cross-legged on the floor near Mack. The story spun out in the wonderful way it always did, and when she reached the end and slowly closed the book, her spirits felt lighter.

"It was a good ending, though I thought for a bit that it might not be," mused Owela.

"I liked the glass slippers and the fairy godmother," said Thomas. "They seemed so grand. How could such things be?"

"It is magic," said Mack. "What is life without magic of one sort or another?"

"The tale," Owela said thoughtfully. "I did like it. I do not read and so would not have been able to learn about it myself. Reading is a sort of magic, is it not?" It was not a skill he had ever needed. He could print his name. His father, Alex Doig, had seen to that, but with no books in their world, what use would it have been to learn to read?

"Well," began Mack, and she smiled at him, "it is not so difficult. Perhaps you may learn some day, if you wish to."

"Yes," he answered. "Perhaps I will."

Mack closed the book and set it back on the shelf. She walked to the port and, rubbing away the condensation on it, peered out and sighed.

"If only we could walk outside for a bit," Mack whispered. Then an idea came to her. The endless rain had finally stopped falling. "Perhaps we can. It is evening. The streets will soon be dark and no one will see us."

"No," Owela replied instantly. "I cannot believe you are saying such a thing. It would not be wise at all. You have forgotten Ben Sparks and his papers, I see. Should I remind you of them?"

Mack wandered restlessly about the cabin. "No, I have not forgotten at all, Owela. It eats at me constantly, but I am sick of being held captive here. You are nearly mad with this confinement as well, if you will only admit it."

"I did tear down as many of the papers as I could find," Thomas reminded them.

"We shall be fine, Owela," soothed Mack. She slipped on her coat. "You have your musket, I will even carry the pistol, and I can run like the wind." She stopped. Lines of concern wrinkled Owela's forehead. "Please," she said quietly. "I will also wear a cape and keep the hood drawn down closely so that no one may see my face or even guess at who I am."

Unwillingly Owela surrendered to her, but his face and voice were serious. "It is against my good judgment, and we will just walk for a few minutes, but yes. And only since I can bear this no longer. We will leave the ship." He picked up his musket from where it leaned against the corner of the cabin. Mack ran out of the room to find her cloak.

"Huzzah!" cheered Jamie, jumping out of his berth and helping Thomas down.

"The pistol? You have it?" Owela asked when Mack returned. She pulled aside her coat to show him the pistol she had thrust into the waist of her breeches. He held out his hand and she gave the weapon to him. He had loaded it himself. It was not cocked and so she could safely carry it this way. Grunting in satisfaction, Owela handed back the pistol.

"I will use it if I must," she promised him. Owela said nothing, remembering with some amusement their first meeting. She had the heart for many things, but not for killing, of that he was certain. No matter. He himself would not hesitate to do anything necessary to protect her.

"It feels almost as though we are going out to a party!" laughed Jamie.

"Well, walking about the damp streets of Boston is hardly my idea of a party, but it certainly will be a change from these last few days," Mack said. In a graceful motion, she swept the cape over her shoulders and pulled up its hood.

Then with Jamie, Thomas, and Owela, Mack left the ship and went out into the late afternoon. It was December 16, 1773, and, oddly enough, a party of a rather different sort awaited them.

CHAPTER ELEVEN

They wandered down the wharf toward the streets of Boston. The rain-washed air felt refreshing to Mack after the closeness of the ship's cabins. Puddles shivered as the wind blew across them, and every person they passed held their cloaks and coats up around their necks. Mack looked out across the water to where other ships were moored at a different wharf. There seemed to be an unusual number of people there. She pulled her hood lower over her face so that no one could see her.

"Let us head this way and go just a little farther. I think I like the look of this street," Jamie said to them over his shoulder. Thomas went ahead of them all, his little legs moving quickly.

"It is good to be out of doors and away from the ship," Owela admitted, breathing in great lungfuls of the air. Not once did his eyes stop scanning the street in search of anyone who paid them too much attention. "But go no farther, Jamie, and let us stay together."

"It is lovely," agreed Mack. The wind snatched at her cape, and so she drew it more closely around herself.

"Do not go so fast, Thomas. I can scarcely keep up. This is supposed to be a walk, not a race," Jamie complained. He puffed and gasped with the brisk pace at which the child was walking.

"Whatever do you mean? That is not running," Thomas cried. "This is!" And suddenly he was racing down the street. Mack ran after him, calling his name, then Jamie and Owela began to run as well. They had nearly gained on her and Thomas, but then Mack and the little boy turned a corner and disappeared.

"Stop!" shouted Owela. "I do not mind the running, but I want you in my sight!"

"Wait for us, you two! Thomas, slow down!" panted Jamie as they rounded the corner themselves.

Mack was sprawled on the ground, rubbing the back of her head. Her hood was down and her hair spilled out to her shoulders. Thomas was watching Mack with a look of misery on his face, and the man into whom she had crashed was just picking himself up. Other men stood behind him, laughing at the collision.

Owela blinked his eyes very hard. Was that war paint he was seeing on the man's face? This was no Native. A Native would never have dressed in such a manner with ragged clothes and a shabby blanket. In spite of the soot-darkened skin highlighted with stripes of red color, this was clearly a citizen of Boston. Then he saw that all the men were similarly dressed. A dozen painted faces stared at his own surprised one.

"Are you hurt, lad?" asked the man in concern. He reached down to pull Mack to her feet. Her hair hung in her eyes, and the seat of her breeches and the back of her cape were soaked. "I fear you will have a goose egg tomorrow, my boy."

"That is no boy, sir," called a familiar voice. The group of men moved apart and Paul Revere stepped forward. "Miss Mack, poor girl. Let me see if you are bleeding. Whatever are you doing out this night? At least you have your loyal friend, Owela, at your side." But there was no anger in his voice, and Mack only heard the same teasing tone he had used with them before.

"I am not really hurt, and I might ask much the same thing of you, Mr. Revere," Mack answered, rubbing the back of her skull where it had struck the road. She eyed with irritation the man who had mistaken her for a boy. He only shrugged his shoulders and smiled an innocent grin. "This looks like quite a gathering."

Revere roared with laughter.

"How right you are, miss," someone shouted. "It will be a special gathering, a fine tea party."

"A tea party? What do you mean, sir?" asked Jamie, who had finally caught his breath.

"Do you see the masts of those ships yonder in Boston harbor?" Revere pointed over to the waterfront. "On several of those ships are hundreds of chests of tea. There has not been a drop of tea consumed in my home or many others in Boston town for quite a while."

Mack already knew this; even the sailors on the ship talked of it. Many people in the colonies were boycotting tea. They would not buy it, nor pay the taxes the Crown had imposed on the drink they so loved.

"But why are you dressed this way?" Mack asked in confusion. What a sight they all were!

Revere puffed out his chest proudly and strutted about in a circle like a rooster.

"Is it not a wonderful disguise? We are Mohawks. This night the Mohawks will dump every chest of tea on those ships into Boston's harbor."

Owela straightened in surprise and looked from man to man. "I cannot believe this. Do you mean to say that from this night on, the tale will be told that Mohawks — people of the Six Nations — did this deed?"

"We hope it shall!" called one of the men.

"Would be a shame if people thought it was us after all the trouble we have taken here," laughed another.

Mack moved forward to put herself between Revere's crowd and Owela. Was he angry? Had he taken insult? She put her hand lightly on his arm. "I think you need not worry. Anyone who sees them will know the truth, Owela. They do not look like Mohawks at all."

"They are dreadful disguises, Mr. Revere," Jamie added cheerfully. "They do not resemble you in the least, Owela. Thank goodness for that."

"Now you have hurt my feelings," teased Revere. "But I have no time to worry about that. The tea calls to us." He motioned to the men that they should carry on to where the ships waited.

"A moment," Owela said with quiet authority. He looked at the men who stood on the wet street, restless and eager with anticipation, their faces dirty and red-smeared. They did look ridiculous. But there was a fire in their eyes that he understood. It was that small spark of freedom of which everyone spoke. It did seem to be growing as quickly as wildfire in the bush on a dry fall day.

"We have a moment," Revere answered pleasantly.

"If the tale will be told that Mohawks did the act, then at least one shall be there to make it true," said Owela. "I am not Mohawk — I am Oneida — but I am one of the Six Nations. My people would not stand with the British in this, I think, for we choose for ourselves how we will live and let none say otherwise. I will do the deed with you. I will take these three back to the ship and then follow."

"You are not leaving us behind," Jamie announced firmly. He squared his shoulders and, drawing himself to his full height, looked up at Owela.

"Nor I!" cried Mack. She met Owela's concerned expression without blinking.

"Where Miss Mack goes, I go," Thomas announced with a wide smile.

"Now, Paul, we cannot take a female into this. What if she faints?" called one of the men in protest. The others murmured amongst themselves.

"Let her come along if she will," said the man into whom Mack had crashed. "She is a big, strong girl. I can speak the truth of that. It was like hitting a wall when she ran into me, and, besides, I have a feeling you boys might faint before she would."

"Good enough," laughed Revere. "You will be in no danger with us around you, Miss Mack." His brows came together briefly as he made his plans, and then he gestured to one of his followers who stood nearby. "There you are, Willy. Run up to the *Odonata* and tell her captain that this pack of revolutionaries is with me. What a story you will have to tell some day, Miss Mack!"

Someone pulled out small pots of paint and sooty grease. Revere smeared their cheeks with black, and they hastily painted each other's faces with red designs. Owela sighed and shook his head. He himself declined the paint — such nonsense was not for him.

"Not that you need it, my boy," shouted Revere, running his eyes over Owela. "You look a wonder!"

Thousands of people stood on the docks and watched as Revere and his crowd approached the ships tied at Griffin's Wharf. Other so-called Mohawks were gathered there; Mack saw more than a hundred eager painted faces. Not a word of protest came from the crews as the men boarded the vessels. There should have been shouting and cheering, but the crowds were quiet. Hundreds of chests of teas were carried up onto the ship's decks and chopped open. One by one, they were dumped with great ceremony into the water. Mack, Jamie, and Owela helped carry the chests while Thomas scampered about watching everything.

By dawn it was all finished. The harbor was littered with wet and sinking cases. A great skiff of tea washed here and there on the water's surface, sticking to the pilings and the hulls of the ships. Weary, but still excited, they all left the vessels and walked onto the crowded wharf.

"We shall march through the streets, my friends," Revere announced to the men. Then he called to Mack and the others, "You revolutionaries will go home to your beds, though. I must insist upon this. Take them back to the ship, Owela, if you will."

"I think I shall sleep very well." Mack stretched and yawned. Her cheeks glowed with all the exertion. She had enjoyed herself so much that she wished there had been three hundred more chests to toss into the harbor. "Good day then, Mr. Revere!" They watched as Revere disappeared into the milling crowd.

"It is a good day. A fine day. I expect it is the most perfect day of my life," said a soft, familiar voice behind her. Mack turned her head slowly. Her happy tiredness evaporated and cold fear crept into her bones, turning her heart to a lump of ice.

"Ben Sparks," she breathed, for there he was, like an awful nightmare from which she could not ever quite awake. Slowly she began to back away until she was at the edge of the wharf.

He had come down to the harbor, drawn by the noise and the large crowd. He might have missed her, but luck had been with him. He was just turning to go, when he saw Jamie, grimy and paint-smeared, leave the ship and walk onto the wharf. A moment later Mack was there before him, and she was a lovely sight indeed. Then it was a simple matter of waiting for her.

Now Jamie turned and saw Sparks leering at Mack. "Run, Mack!" Jamie cried. "It is Ben Sparks, Owela!"

The moment he heard Jamie call the warning, Sparks

darted forward. Owela raised his musket and aimed at the man who was rushing toward Mack. "Move, Mack!" he shouted frantically. Jamie pushed Thomas out of the way.

Mack instantly thought of the pistol, but before she could even reach for it, Sparks pulled the weapon from her waist and thrust it into his belt. His other hand closed in a painful grip around her wrist.

"Yes, it is me, and I can see just how you have missed Ben Sparks all this while, my chick. But that is done and we shall be together once more. What fine times we two will have. I have made many plans for us these last days, you should know." Jamie and Thomas edged toward Sparks who kept his eyes fastened on Owela.

"Let her go if you have any thought at all for your life," Owela warned in barely controlled anger. "Let her go now, I say!"

Sparks turned in surprise at the sound of Owela's voice. There was a scuffling sound. Jamie hurled himself between Mack and Sparks, trying to pull her away. "Leave her alone, you animal!" he cried. Sparks swatted at him and knocked him to the ground, and then, with a quick jerk, pulled Mack in front of himself. She fought Sparks hard. Jamie picked himself up off of the ground, blood pouring from his nose.

"Shoot me, will you?" Sparks taunted Owela. "But would you shoot through her to do it? I am fond of this girl, but not as fond as I am of my own skin." People all around them started to sidle away in fear that they might be shot themselves. Sparks raised his voice. "See now what this Native is about to do to an innocent man and his woman! Why, I am only claiming what is mine, as you may tell. Have none of you seen my notices posted all over Boston's walls?" There were quick nods and murmurs of agreement. Yes, some had seen that very paper.

"Let go of me, Ben Sparks!" Mack screamed. "You are a thief and a liar and I am no more your servant than you are mine!"

"Take your hands from her, I say, or it will cost you your life," Owela said in a deadly, calm voice. He knew the crowd was watching him. He knew how it must look to them to see a Native threatening a white man. He did not care. His finger was a steady and growing pressure upon the musket's trigger. Mack would not be taken by Sparks, and it did not matter what the cost might be to himself.

"Oh, you are correct there, Miss Mack, my love. Of course, you are not my servant," Sparks whispered, watching Owela closely. Jamie stood near him, blood heedlessly dripping from his nose. Then Sparks shouted loudly, "This woman is my wife, and forty shillings will go to the man who shoots the Native so I may be on my way back home with her!" Without taking his eyes from Owela, he slowly kissed Mack's cheek. Mack cried out in horror and struggled against him.

"Let her go! Let her go!" shrieked Thomas, who could no longer stand the sight of Jamie bleeding and Mack held in the foul man's hands. He dropped down to the ground and bit Sparks' ankle as hard as he could.

"You filthy little beast!" cried Sparks, and he loosened

his grip just a bit. He kicked Thomas. With a sob the boy fell back away from the edge of the wharf.

In a hot flood, Mack's fear left her. She wrenched her arms from Sparks' hold. She turned and her eyes met those of Ben Sparks for an instant. Then with every bit of her strength, she pushed against his chest and sent him off balance. He tumbled backward into Boston harbor's dirty water with a resounding splash. There was a pattering of applause from a few watchers. Owela and Jamie rushed to Mack's side.

"Run now!" cried Owela. He picked up Thomas and carried him.

They ran through the crowd until they reached the wharf where *Odonata* lay. Was Ben Sparks following them? Would he see where they went? Owela took one last hard, angry look for Sparks before he followed them aboard. He could hear Captain Apple loudly exclaiming over Jamie's bloody face.

"Come below, Jamie." Mack's voice was weary. "I will see to your nose."

When Owela entered the cabin a while later, she was still dabbing at Jamie's face. A pitcher, rags, and a bowl of bloodied water were on the table beside her. "He will follow. I know it," Mack said shakily. "And your poor nose, Jamie. It is broken, I think."

"Let me see." Owela felt Jamie's nose carefully. "Not a break, only a bruising, my friend. Your handsome looks will remain as they were."

"It would have been worse than that had you not bit

Sparks," Mack said to Thomas. She hugged the child closely to her. "You are such a brave boy, Thomas, my dear."

"You were most amazing, Thomas," Jamie agreed, breathing through his mouth. "And you did wonderfully, Owela, as well."

Owela stood very still. His face was blank, but inside he was filled with anger at himself that he had been so foolish. They should never have gone out into the city and certainly should not have joined Revere's party. It had given him such an odd pleasure to see Mack laughing and happy even for that little while, though. But the cost. It had brought Sparks upon her!

Mack could not meet Owela's eyes. "I know you will say it is my fault," she said quietly, rubbing a hand over her face. She turned and gently touched Jamie's nose. "It is my fault. Ben Sparks will find us again."

Owela shook his head slowly. "Whether Sparks followed us is of no concern to me. I spoke with the captain as I passed him and he has armed the crew. Sparks cannot come aboard, and when Revere hears of what has happened, he will stand up for you as he said he would. Sparks will be arrested."

"I must believe that. If I do not, I think I shall go mad," she said weakly. Mack picked up a clean rag, dipped it in the pitcher, and scrubbed hard at her face where Sparks had kissed her. "Thank you once more, Owela," came her low voice.

The reminder of what he had seen the man do

strained Owela's control. "Put Ben Sparks from your mind. Let me worry about him. Although, it is he who should be worried."

"You are all covered in blood, Jamie. It looks a sight," Thomas observed with great interest. "I had no idea a person had so much blood in them."

"Well, I have less now than a few moments ago," Jamie said in a cross voice. "It is most uncomfortable. And I have something stuck in my moccasins to make it even worse."

Jamie pulled off his moccasins and dropped them to the floor. Then he broke into loud laughter. Owela looked down. Jamie's moccasins were full of tea.

"Let us save it," Jamie suggested. "We shall make a pact. When we are all old, we will brew it up and drink the tea to remember this day on some special occasion. It will be merry!"

"Done," vowed Mack, who was grasping at anything to forget what had happened. She found a glass bottle and carefully poured the tea into it. Mack tried to think ahead all those years. What would they be doing then?

"But right now I am thoroughly chilled, Mack," Jamie moaned. "Thomas is as well and look at Owela! He is near to perishing with the cold." Owela looked doubtful at this. Cold? Hardly.

"We will not drink the tea, but what would you have? Coffee? Chocolate?" Mack asked him. She shrugged out of the heavy cape and rubbed her hands together briskly.

"No," Jamie decided slowly. "I think a small tot of Madeira would do us all well. Only a bit now and thoroughly mixed with water, if you must insist. As I know very well that you shall. You will like this, Thomas."

"Well," she said reluctantly, as she took three goblets from a shelf. "If it is not a strong mixture, then perhaps just a little. Thomas, though, shall have cider." She filled a mug with cider for Thomas. Mack poured small portions of Madeira into the goblets and then added a generous amount of water.

"Come now, Mack, this is far too weak. We will not even be able to taste it," scolded Jamie as he watched her pour. Then he took the bottle from her hand to top up his own glass. "Can you think of any reason why the party should end? Let us celebrate the fact that the fishes have perhaps eaten Ben Sparks." He linked his arms through Thomas's and swung him around in a wild, clumsy dance as the liquid sloshed around in the goblet he held.

"Are you daft?" Mack asked him. "This is not in the least funny!" Still, he looked so silly, she began to laugh.

"No, I am not daft at all, and you two must dance as well. It is a dance of celebration!" Jamie gave a wild whoop and began to sing some nonsense song.

"I think not," said Owela as he watched the performance. He knew music and dancing. There were drums at the Castle and there were the old songs of his people. All his life he had danced at ceremonies or at celebrations of the return of victorious warriors. But this! How strange and different Mack's world was from his if this was how they celebrated a safe homecoming.

Jamie took a great gulp of the strong drink and swallowed hard. With a sputter he gasped and choked, spraying Madeira across the cabin, laughter and wine mixing dreadfully in his throat.

"Jamie MacNeil," called someone loudly from the doorway. "If your sister, Jane, could see you, she would have your head." Jamie turned, his eyes filled with tears, the spirits splashing from the goblet to the cabin floor. John MacNeil crossed the cabin in a few strides, thumped his brother on the back, and then stood there shaking his head hopelessly. "I rather think you have been away from home just a bit too long, my boy."

CHAPTER TWELVE

"John!" Jamie clutched his brother's arm. "Samuel! My word, you have found us at last!"

"That we have," Samuel said happily. "It was no small thing chasing you across the woods of New York, but with our expert tracking skills you would not have eluded us much longer. Besides, the three trappers we came upon were most cooperative in answering our questions about you — after a bit of coaxing, that is. They told us what happened on the beach at Fort Niagara. When it was clear that you had not been taken south, we backtracked and headed east."

John embraced his brother and, for several seconds, the cabin was quiet. Then he lifted his face from his brother's shoulder and looked over at Mack. Her eyes were bright with tears of happiness.

"Elias Stack met us and brought word that you were safe and with Owela," John explained. "You have him to thank." John then turned his attention to Owela. "But you have my gratitude as well, my friend. What I owe you cannot ever be repaid."

"It was my pleasure to help you and your family, John," Owela replied. "A most interesting task, my friend," he added dryly. He reached inside his shirt and began to pull the locket over his head.

"You must keep it," John insisted. "Perhaps it will remind you of this adventure now and again."

Owela smiled. "I suspect it will."

John released Jamie and opened his arms to Mack. She crossed the room, put her hands on his shoulders, and kissed his unshaven cheek. He, in turn, wrapped his arms around her and held her in a tight embrace, his eyes shut in relief that she and Jamie were safe.

From the circle of his arms Mack said in a small voice, "You found us. I thought we might not ever see you again." She pulled away just a bit, and, slipping the silver ring from her finger, gave it to John.

He put the ring on his smallest finger. "Ah, yes," he laughed softly, "the ring did its work for you, as I knew it would."

"John," Mack went on, swallowing hard. "We have a new person among us. May I present young Thomas? It is just Thomas, you must understand. He is one of us now and must remain so. It is a very long story and one I think I am not up to at the moment. Jamie, I truly think we might have just a bit more of that Madeira after all."

There were so many things to talk about, from their travels across the countryside to Boston to what they would do now. John and Samuel would need to rest for a day or so, but then they would all have to leave Boston as soon as possible. The city was definitely unsafe territory after the tea party.

"The Crown and Parliament will not take this from the colonies," said John bluntly. He set down his glass of Madeira and walked uneasily about the cabin, twisting the ring round and round his finger in a habit very familiar to Mack. "There will be some sort of retaliation. You can stake your life on it." He stopped and looked at them. "*Odonata* will sail in a few days. I will give the orders to Captain Apple this evening, for I would have her away to England before there is any trouble and she cannot leave Boston at all."

Mack felt herself go quite still and cold inside. "We will be on her, I suppose?" she asked hesitantly. She swallowed, her throat dry, as she waited for his answer.

John looked at Mack and Jamie. "Everything has changed now, hasn't it?" he asked softly. "You must make your choice on this, my dears. If you return to England, at least I will know you are safe with Jane and her family. You know that nothing would make me happier than to take you both home to the island. As your older brother and guardian I have the right to decide for you both, but neither of you is a child any longer, particularly after what you have experienced." The muscles in his jaws clenched as he fought to control his rage over their suffering. "I leave the decision to you."

"You would be with us, would you not, John?" Jamie asked hesitantly. "You would come back to Brierly, as well?"

"No," John said gently. "Brierly is not my home. I had said that I would go with you when the time came for you to return, but all that has changed. If war reaches

Canada — and it may — then I must be there to protect the home I have made for myself. Would you be willing to face that prospect?" He searched their faces before he went on. "I will send you safely back to England if that is what you choose, but I must stay here. Samuel and I will return to Pêche Island."

"If we sail back to England, we will remain there for a long while. I know it," Mack whispered. "We will have not the shred of an idea of when we might see you again." Her eyes flicked to Owela, who was watching her intently. "Or our friends here."

"If you do choose to stay here with me, I cannot say when you will see Brierly and the family again," John warned her. "It could be many years, for this would no longer be simply a visit to Canada. You would have to make your life here, as I do. I believe you have seen that it is not such an easy or safe task at times. You must understand that I cannot offer you the luxuries of Brierly."

Mack lifted her shoulders and laughed. "Luxuries? Oh, John, I will stay here with you. To return to the island and live there quietly will be all the luxury I ever need. You and Jamie are my family."

"Jamie? What of you?" asked John. His eyes met those of his young brother.

"I stay as well, John," said Jamie firmly. "How could I possibly leave Mack here to her own devices? How would you survive alone with her? And Natka and Wallace. What a surprise it will give them when we return after all." Owela made a snorting noise and Samuel laughed out loud at that. Mack merely ignored

Jamie's teasing. She was too happy to let him annoy her.

"So be it then," said John, very pleased that they would go home with him. He sat once more and refilled his goblet with Madeira. Then he turned the talk to other more serious matters. "This man, Ben Sparks. The trappers told us about him, although they clearly did not wish to do so. I had not known of him, but I vow that I will not ever forget his name and what he has done to those dear to me."

There was a grim determination in John's voice that Mack had never heard before. She shivered a little and reached out to where Thomas had stood just a moment ago. He was not there. The door of the cabin was slightly opened. He must have slipped out while they were talking. She felt a sudden thrill of panic and, without a word, she left and went out onto the deck.

"He said he had to get the rest of the papers down, whatever that might mean," a sailor told her. Mack grew pale and the man, seeing her stricken look, hastened to reassure her. "He is naught but a street child, miss. He will know his way around in a way not many others might, and he will be back here in no time at all."

John insisted that Mack, Jamie, and Owela get some rest. They had been up all night and were quite done in. "Sleep," he said. "Samuel and I will search for him. It is likely he will come back to the ship before we do." But Thomas did not return that afternoon, nor in the evening. When John and Samuel stepped back on board the ship after a long search later that night, they had not found the little boy.

"Something has happened to him. I know it," Mack said, fighting back the burning tears.

"You cannot be certain of that," John comforted her. "He is an orphan child, my dear. He has lived all his life in the streets on his own. He may have just decided to take up that way of life once again."

"No, I tell you, John! He did not wish to leave us here. He wanted to be with me. I wanted so much to help him, just like Jamie and I were helped. He is only a little boy —" her voice trailed off and without another word Mack went to her cabin.

Two days later they were still arguing, for Mack and Jamie would not leave Boston without Thomas. There was nothing to be done, John insisted. They had searched the city and not a trace had been seen of him.

John was becoming more and more anxious to leave the city and to send *Odonata* back to England. "Paul Revere has left Boston, but I have spoken to some of his friends. For your sake they will make certain the child is searched for, and, if Thomas is found, they will send him to you at the island. Or I shall return myself, no matter what is happening between England and Boston. You have my word on it," John said. He saw Mack's desperate expression and he went on. "I think there is no time to linger here. War will come. I have seen what that is like."

"I have not seen war, but I know how it feels to lose one you care for. You do also," Mack said to him. "It can break your heart."

John rubbed his hand across his forehead. He then crossed the room and stood in front of the windows at the stern of the *Odonata*, staring out at Boston's dark harbor. Lanterns shone from ships anchored all around them. Condensation dripped down the cold glass like tears.

"Yes. It can break your heart," John answered simply. His eyes shifted to Samuel who sat in the cabin's shadows with Owela and Jamie. "There was someone once. She was my friend, Samuel's sister. Sometimes I still dream of her and the happy times we had." Mack left the desk and walked slowly to John. Ripples from the reflection of the lanterns at the stern of *Odonata* played across her face. She took his hand in hers.

"We have both lost so much. My parents and your father and David, all taken at the same time. I cannot bear anything like that again. I would not lose Thomas — he has become so dear to me. I cannot stand the thought of him going through what Jamie and I did. Help find him. Please." John looked at her.

"We will find him. I promise you this, Mack, but for now we must return to Pêche Island. Even Niagara will not be far enough. Do not think me cruel," he said gently. "I know what the child means to you, but there is Sparks to consider, as well, not to mention the threat of war. We leave in the morning and the ship will sail. There will be no more discussion of it."

Mack nodded. He was correct, she knew. He was always correct. She felt herself chafe a bit at the gentle hold this man had over her.

There was much to do. They had to prepare their gear and make certain they had proper clothing for winter travel. John and Samuel wore *souliers de boeuf*, high moccasins of heavy leather that would protect their feet and calves in the snow. For the rest there would be shoe-paks, moccasins with a bit of wool blanket cut and fitted into them to keep their feet warm. As well, they would wrap and tie wool about the lower parts of their legs against the cold.

"Will our coats be enough?" Jamie asked John while they sorted through their gear on their last night on the ship. "They are of heavy cloth, but in truly cold weather I think we may freeze."

Owela pulled a blanket from Mack's bunk. He turned to her and inclined his head. "Might I show you something with this?"

"Of course," she answered, then burst into hearty laughter as Owela flung the blanket over Jamie's head. Jamie threw up his arms in surprise.

"Be still, now," Owela commanded. "If you wiggle, I cannot show you how to make a matchcoat. A rope or a piece of leather, if you will," Owela said over his shoulder to Mack. Mack poked about in a trunk, then pulled out a length of line. She handed it to Owela.

"I am smothering," Jamie complained from under the blanket.

"Stick your arms out to the side," Owela ordered. Pulling the blanket back a bit, Owela drew the two sides forward beneath Jamie's arms and around his waist. He tugged the blanket into position and then tied it closed with the rope. Then he folded the fabric back from Jamie's face into a hood.

"You look like a friar," laughed Mack.

"You will need a pin to fasten it shut here. It will keep you warm enough," Owela said, adjusting the fit.

"I believe it will," Jamie puffed. "I must get it off or die of the heat." He undid the line and passed the blanket to Mack, who folded it and placed it back on her bunk.

"All is ready," Owela said. He sat on Mack's bunk. "We have our weapons, powder, ball, and shot. There are snowshoes for us all. We will carry jerky and parched corn, peas and some flour."

"That is all the food we will carry?" Mack asked in surprise. "We shall starve."

"We will not starve any more than we will freeze," Owela told her. "We will hunt along the way, as we did before."

"Ah!" cried John. "I can hear the knees of every squirrel in the forest knocking." Then he turned to Mack. "You must learn to handle a musket as well. With enough blankets and a canvas fly to shelter you at night, Mack, we will manage."

"You will see Mack does well on the trail," Owela said quietly to John. His gaze rested on Mack. "She can shoot. She kept the pace I set with not a word of complaint. Oh, she must have her hot water for washing and a tea and a warm meal in her belly each evening, but I do not think you will find that it is such a bother."

"We will live like kings!" laughed John. "Sleep well, then." He and Jamie went off, leaving Mack and Owela alone in the cabin. All at once the room became very quiet.

"Well, then," she said aimlessly. Owela fingered the silver locket he still wore around his neck. The bed, slung from heavy ropes from the ship's deck head, creaked and swayed.

"Well, then," he said in answer. "I am to my rest. Sleep well, Mack, and do not worry about the child, Thomas. He is far more able to take care of himself than you think." Then he padded across the cabin soundlessly in his moccasins. As the door shut, it made a sharp snick. Suddenly her cabin seemed very large and empty.

Mack let her breath out slowly. So much had happened so quickly. She stripped off her clothing, dropped it to a chair, and slipped a nightdress down over her head, smoothing the fabric and pulling the sleeves down. It would be the last time in a long while that she would sleep in a nightdress in a proper bed. For the next few weeks she would sleep in her clothing. Bed would be a blanket on the frozen ground. If she was lucky, she might wash her face and hands once a day.

She walked across the cabin and climbed into the berth. It swayed a bit, rocking her like a baby in its cradle. She pulled the goose down quilt up over her shoulders and breathed in once, very deeply. Slowly Mack let the breath leave her lungs. She would think no more, not of the tea party or poor little Thomas or the long journey to Pêche Island. Her eyes closed and she slept. And when she woke in the morning, it was to the sounds of a ship preparing to set sail for England.

CHAPTER THIRTEEN

"Jane, I cannot possibly leave Mack," Jamie explained as he wrote in his dreadful, blotchy style. He sat at a table quickly scribbling out a message to his sister before they set off on their journey that morning. *Odonata* would carry letters back to England from John and Mack, as well. "She does get into the most dreadful fixes, and John truly needs my assistance as well. You have absolutely no idea how they depend on me, Jane. Besides, think of how interesting we will be when we finally do return to England. Imagine how it will be when you take us to Court after all the exciting times we are having here! The King will be stunned at how colorful we have all become."

Mack stared at the blank page in front of her. She had a good idea that Jamie was spouting his usual cheery nonsense. She, however, had a far more difficult task.

"By the time you read this, Jane, let your heart rest easy, for we will be safe with John at his home," Mack wrote, choosing the words carefully as she explained what had happened. "I know you have saved every letter that John sent to you when he was a boy in Canada. Can you recall how you longed to be part of that adventure, how you thought you might come here some day yourself? In the end you made other choices and you are very happy. Henry might say it is foolishness, but I think you will understand, Jane.

"I must make my own decision about how I shall live my life. I have made friends here, friends who have become quite dear to me. If it comes to pass that I have done the wrong thing in staying in Canada, I will have only myself to blame. I would rather make that mistake than let someone make another for me." As she wrote these words, Mack felt a great weight leave her heart. She had made her decision and, despite the pain she knew it would cause Jane, it was the right one.

Owela waited in silence, watching as they wrote their words on the paper. When they were finished, John folded the letters, slipped them into a document packet, and sealed the flap shut with wax. Then picking up their packs and weapons, they all left the cabin to join Samuel on deck.

Owela walked behind Mack. "You chose wisely," he said to her back. She stopped and faced him.

"Yes, I did," she answered in a clear voice.

"You will have a good life with John and Jamie."

"I think so. I love them both very much."

Owela looked away. "And that will be enough for you?"

"It must be enough," Mack said, blinking in surprise. "It is exactly what I wanted. What else might I possibly need?"

Owela began to answer, but then John called down, "Come along, you two. The ship is about to set sail and we must be off."

"Well, we had better leave this ship or it will sail off with you on it, after all. And me also!" Owela said lightly, and she laughed with him as they made their way to the deck.

Goodbyes and God speeds said, Mack went with the others to the wharf and watched the sailors cast off. Slowly *Odonata* left Boston with the outgoing tide, just as the sun was coming up above the ocean. Mack would never forget the way the ship looked as the crew raised the sails and the vessel leaned ponderously to the rising breeze.

They left the wharf and headed down the street away from the harbor. John and Jamie walked ahead of the others. Mack followed, while Owela and Samuel took up the rear. There would be shifting in the procession, regrouping as conversations changed, but Mack would always be in the center, the armed men around her. Mack had a pistol and Jamie carried a musket that John had taken from *Odanata*'s armory. Jamie shifted the weapon about, trying to become accustomed to its weight in his hands or in his arms. Mack looked around carefully, searching the streets one last time. She was so happy to be staying here with John and Jamie, but the thought of Thomas filled her heart with a terrible sadness. With a deep sigh of resignation she left Boston

◇ ◇

"Is that a tear I see rolling down your face? Oh goodness me, it is!" Ben Sparks whispered sarcastically. He laughed softly and his chuckling was filled with menace. He stood in the shadows of an alley with Thomas at his side. "And I thought you would like to see your friends depart, you ungrateful boy."

Thomas could not answer Sparks. A dirty twist of rag was tied across his mouth, his hands were bound, and a rope of coarse hemp was tied around his neck. Thomas stared as Mack and Jamie walked away from him. Tears ran down his face and soaked the rag.

"Goodbye, Miss Mack. Goodbye," Sparks said in a singsong voice that made Thomas's skin crawl. "Come along now, my fine chick. It's a hard route we will be taking so that we do not cross paths with your friends. I think you will fetch me a pretty penny from the Natives. You will find life amongst them rather different than anything your precious Miss Mack might have shown you." Giving the rope a quick jerk, Ben Sparks led him away.

◇ ◇

For more than a week they walked out into the countryside. Long stretches of forest spread out all around them. They were following the same route that Mack and Jamie had traveled with Ben Sparks and then with Owela, only in reverse. John set a lively pace for he wanted to make good use of the clear weather. Christmas came and went quickly, with no time to properly mark it.

Each day squirrels, woodcock, or grouse were added

to a pot or roasted over a fire in the evening. The wind was light but brisk, and a weak sun shone through patchy clouds. At night the moon was a sickle of ivory that slowly grew larger and wider. On a few mornings, the branches of the bare trees and thick bushes were lightly dusted with snow. They did not stop in Albany, since there were enough supplies and the hunting was good. This time Mack felt no resentment. They were going home to John's island and surely no more misfortunes would befall them. Only the thought of Thomas lingered sadly in Mack's mind.

One cold morning Mack found herself stepping carefully through the fallen leaves and small branches. The leather soles of her moccasins had become slippery. It would be easy to take a fall. She kept her eyes to the forest's floor, glancing up now and again.

Jamie and Owela walked on ahead of her. "It will be good to see Fort Detroit and the island once more," Jamie tossed back over his shoulder. "We are making excellent time, right John? I can scarcely believe this weather and how fine it has been for the end of December."

"I can only pray it holds," John remarked from his spot at the end of the line. "If not, we must winter at Niagara. We will be there in a week or so, I hope, if you can bear up."

"I can, John. And, either way, I cannot wait to show you the island, Owela," Jamie went on. His breath rose in faint puffs from his lips. "John's house is wonderful. It has such a perfect view of the river. And the apple trees are so beautiful in the spring."

"My sister, Marie, and I had a camp on the very spot when we were children," Samuel added wistfully. "What times we had!"

"Oh, I will not go as far as Detroit, Jamie," said Owela quietly. "We are but a day or so from the Oneida Castle, my village, and it is there I will leave you to go on by yourselves."

A small, icy shock hit Mack in the stomach. Jamie, as well, seemed stunned. "I had thought we would be together a while longer," he said unhappily.

"I truly would enjoy that," Owela answered. "But it is my home, you see. My family is there. Perhaps you might all stay a few days and visit with us?" He looked steadily at Mack. "I think you would see it is a very good place, a place where a person can live in contentment."

"We cannot afford a long stay, Owela, if we are to make Niagara as soon as I hope to," John said. "We will spend tomorrow night there with you."

That night Mack lay wrapped in her blankets, facing the low fire that flickered in the darkness. Above her stretched the canvas fly that each evening John insisted on erecting for her and Jamie. Jamie lay curled with his back against Mack's. John and Samuel were snoring lumps only a few feet away.

Only Owela was not asleep. It was his watch. John had decided from the first that they would take turns keeping watch throughout the night. Nothing had threatened, but they were in the wilderness and care must be taken. At first Mack had felt a prickle of irritation that she had not been included in the watches, but she realized that she had no true skill with the pistol she carried. The job was best left to those who could do it. Still, some nights, unable to sleep, she would crawl from her bed and sit by the low fire to talk with whoever was on watch.

Mack was wide awake. Carefully, so she would not wake Jamie, she sat up. She left one blanket around him and gathered the other about her shoulders. Owela watched her make her way around the low flame. She dropped to the ground next to him, where he sat on a chunk of wood, and leaned back against it. For a while they said nothing.

Mack broke the silence. "You will be happy to see your family, then," she whispered softly. "You have not ever said much of them or of your village." She pulled the blanket beneath her so she would feel less of the cold forest floor, then pulled it up around herself.

"Yes," Owela answered. His musket lay across his knees and a blanket was draped over his shoulders. "It has been months since I have been home, though word would have reached there that I am safe." Mack looked up at him. He chuckled softly. "There is not much that happens here that the Oneida do not learn of in time, you see." The firelight flickered upon his skin, and the tattoos running along his jawbone stood out sharply. There was a distant look in Owela's eyes.

"I, too, will be happy to return to something ordinary and peaceful again," Mack said, closing her eyes and turning her face to the fire. "Is it peaceful at the Castle?"

"It is a safe and peaceful place, but it is not only that," Owela said. He seemed to struggle for the words at first, but then his quiet voice went steadily on. "It is the way of things there that I miss the most. The drums and the singing at night and the dancing. There was music in Boston, the fiddles and such that I could hear in the taverns as we passed in the street, but it is not the same at all as what is done at the Castle. The sound of it stirs the blood.

"Then there is the food. Even it has a different taste when eaten there, when you have taken the animal yourself, and it has been cooked by the women in the longhouse. It may not be served on fine plates of china such as you had on the ship, but there is not a thing better than to sit near the fire and share a meal with those you love and then go to your rest. The longhouse is like a creature wrapped around you. It is like your ship in that way, I suppose. So many people all of the same clan may all sleep within it and yet, in your own cubicle, you are alone."

Owela blinked his eyes sharply and looked down at Mack. What must she think of his sentimental ramblings? Mack, though, was asleep. Her head had fallen a little to one side, and her breathing was so quiet that he could barely see the rise and fall of her chest.

If he had been alone, Owela would have let the fire die to coals, but the night was growing colder. He carefully leaned forward and placed several sticks upon the flames. Then, taking the blanket from his shoulders, he gently spread it over Mack. She mumbled something under her breath, rolled to her side, and squirmed a bit to make a spot in the leaves.

When she woke in the morning, Owela's place had

been taken by John. The sun was just coming up and the strangely wavering clouds that hung in the sky were tinted pink. A mackerel sky, she thought as she stretched and stared at the clouds with a sailor's eye. We will have rain soon or maybe snow. John smiled down at her. He tossed branches onto the fire and set a pot of water to boil for tea.

"Will it be a wet night tonight?" he asked her. She sat up and pulled leaves from her hair.

"I expect so. I may be glad of that canvas fly if it is." Mack stood and pulled her clothing into order. She picked up her bedding to shake it out and roll it and then saw the second blanket. It was Owela's, she knew. He must have spent a cold night.

The rest of the camp was stirring, and John made no attempt to move quietly. They lost precious minutes of daylight with morning meals, so he insisted they rise early. There was no grumbling from Mack.

"I will help when I return from the bushes," she said to John.

"Owela is out there," John told her.

She waited until she saw Owela walking back to the fire. Then she made her way toward the bushes just beyond the camp. The men cared nothing for their privacy. It was only the presence of a female amongst them that caused them to be the least bit delicate about what they might otherwise have done in the open. Bushes were often the only concealment to be had, but even hidden behind the thick foliage of rhododendrons, Mack knew she was not ever alone.

"You may go out beyond the camp a ways when nature calls you to do so," John had told her bluntly, "but one of us will always be on the watch."

As Owela neared her, Mack called, "Good morning!"

"A good morning indeed," he answered. "Though we may get wet in the afternoon. Did you sleep well?"

"I did. I was warm and cozy with the extra blanket."

Owela cleared his throat. "That is good to know." He smiled at her. "Go on, now. I will wait here."

When they returned to the camp, everyone was up. John and the others were putting their gear into order. Jamie had shot at a rabbit yesterday afternoon; he was cleaning his musket under John's watchful scrutiny. There was hot tea. The smell of it made Mack's mouth water.

"You should see yourself, Mack," said Samuel.

"You had better wash your face!" teased Jamie. "You have a great smear of dirt on your cheek. Were you rolling in the mud last night?"

John turned away to hide the grin he could not control, but Mack and Owela kept their expressions carefully blank. Mack took a square of fabric from her pouch and poured hot water on it, then wiped her cheeks and hands. That would have to do since they were readying to leave.

"We are close to the Castle," said Owela. He hoisted his pack across his shoulders and settled it comfortably.

"Let us set out," John answered, picking up his musket and document case. "If we press on as quickly as we can, we may reach the Castle before darkness and shelter there for the night."

They put out the fire. Mack looked around the campsite, making certain nothing was left behind. Then they began to walk. The sun was well up now but clouds were starting to move in. As their party passed through the woods, Mack could hear jays and cardinals calling through the tall trees. Now and then a swoop of red or deep blue flitted through the branches.

John pushed them on. They had only one brief stop in late morning. Although the air was cold, sweat gleamed on their faces. By afternoon a thick layer of clouds covered the sky, and the sun was but a dim halo of light. There was little talk now. A sense of urgency as sharp as the scent of musk could be felt along with the rising wind.

Mack pulled her matchcoat more closely around her. The wind whipped strands of her hair from under its hood. When she pushed back the hood to brush the hair back from her eyes, she felt the chilled air go down her neck. By late afternoon it had begun to snow. The flakes were huge and wet; patters of rain splashed around them and the ground grew slushy and slippery. Their clothing became damp, then wet.

John called a stop. "We could camp here beneath these trees." A steep hill rose a little behind him. The brush and large oak trunks might give some shelter. "It would not be so bad, I think. But how much farther to the Castle, Owela?" John asked.

Owela set the butt of his musket on the ground and ran a hand over his face. "Not so far. Three miles. Maybe four."

"We must go on, I think," Mack said breathlessly. "If I rest for just a few minutes I shall get my wind."

John patted her shoulder. "Good enough. You will be glad of it once you are in a longhouse instead of under a tree in the forest this night. Jamie, Owela, go on to the top of this rise to see how the land lays, if you will."

Mack settled on the ground next to where Samuel was squatting.

"You are going to have a wet *derriere*," Samuel warned.

She felt the wet soak into the seat of her breeches, but she was so tired she did not care. For a moment there was a break in the clouds, and shafts of sunlight shot like spears into the forest's gloom. She shaded her eyes and looked up to where Jamie and Owela had just disappeared into the trees that swayed above them.

"It does not seem so bad," Jamie said a bit later to Owela as they stood at the edge of the ridge. The trees were thinner here and the land flatter. Once they were past the ridge, the going would be easier.

"It is like this the rest of the way," Owela said. Then he stopped talking. His eyes narrowed.

"What is it?" asked Jamie and he followed Owela's gaze. There, where the trees thinned and the forest opened, was a man. His face was shadowed, but the brief pass of sunlight glinted off his musket. Jamie and Owela stood motionless. The man raised his hand in greeting. Owela let out a great sigh of breath and he laughed softly.

"Do you know him?" asked Jamie, squinting. Snow had again begun to fall as the sunlight disappeared. "Is it someone from the Castle? How in the world can you tell who it is?"

"I would know that fellow anywhere," Owela told him. "It is my father, Alex Doig." Owela lifted his arm and waved to the man who had started out toward them.

"Your father?" Jamie raised his musket in greeting and stepped closer to the edge.

"Have an eye, Jamie. The footing is slippery here," said Owela. He looked back at his father, who began to run purposefully toward them.

Owela turned to Jamie, but Jamie was not there. Owela heard a scream of pain and felt himself go cold and still. Cries of alarm came from where Mack and the others were waiting. Owela looked down along the edge of the bluff. There lay Jamie in a crumpled pile, his musket in the snow nearby, his leg bent beneath him at an odd angle.

CHAPTER FOURTEEN

With his knife, John carefully cut away the fabric of Jamie's breeches. The fair skin of his brother's leg became covered in goose bumps in the cold. John looked down at the ugly, red bruise and broken skin of Jamie's thigh.

"It is a clean break, I think, but a break nonetheless," John said with grim concern. Jamie lay motionless and white-faced. His forehead was beaded with sweat, and melting slush dripped from his clothing. Mack gently brushed at it, tears in her eyes.

The bone of his thigh had snapped when he had fallen, arms pin-wheeling, to slide partway down the bluff and slam into a tree. Jamie had been conscious when they carried him the rest of the way down, but the pain from the grating ends of the bones had been too much and he had fainted. They now knelt or stood around his blanket-shrouded body. Mack held Jamie's head in her lap.

"What can we do?" Her voice trembled, although she fought to keep it steady. She could not bear the thought of Jamie's pain.

"The poor lad," grumbled Alex Doig. "We shall carry him to the Castle, lass, do not fret now. The women there will heal his leg." He turned to his son and swept his eyes up and down over the young man. "And just how are you, Owela?" He pulled Owela into his arms in a bone-cracking hug.

"I am well, Da." Owela returned the embrace with all his heart.

John leaned over and stroked his brother's cheek. Jamie could have been killed. They could deal with a broken leg. Rising to his feet, John squeezed Alex's shoulder. "It is good to see you, my friend."

"And you also, John," answered Alex. "How good it is that you have come back to the Castle once again." Jamie groaned and Mack bent over him, murmuring comfort.

"We will build a *travois* and carry him the rest of the way," John said wearily. "His leg must be kept very still. We must find large branches for the *travois* and small branches for a splint. Make certain that they are straight, Samuel. I will splint the bone myself."

Mack was relieved, at least, that Jamie was unconscious, so he would not have to endure the agonizing pain of having the bone set. Just to be certain, however, Alex and Owela held him down while John splinted the leg. Jamie moaned faintly just once. Then from saplings and the canvas fly, they fashioned a *travois*, which they would use as a stretcher. They carefully set Jamie upon it and lay his and their weapons next to him. Mack spread another blanket across his motionless form before John and Alex lifted the stretcher.

They picked their way slowly through the forest, stepping carefully on the wet leaves and slushy, slippery moss. The sleet had changed to snow now, and a blustery wind rushed through the trees. The branches groaned.

"This does change things," John thought out loud. "I see now we shall not simply stop at the Castle. We must winter there and go no farther." There was the slightest edge of concern in his voice.

Owela reassured him, "Do not fear, John. You are all welcome in our lodge. My da adopted the ways of my mam's people as he had to if he were to marry among us. We are of the wolf clan and our sense of family is strong. You are as near to being family as you can be."

"Is it a large family?" asked Mack. She looked down at Jamie, who appeared to be resting comfortably as they walked. He was quiet now, his face sheltered from the snow by a blanket.

A rumble of laughter rose from Alex. "Large? Might you call thirty or so people all in one building large, lass?"

"A family of thirty!" Mack looked back at Owela. "How many cousins have you?"

"I do not have so many cousins, and it is not all family as such. The clan is what ties us together," Owela explained. "My da has always said that the Oneida and the Scots have much in common. The clans, the breechcloth being so much like a kilt, the chieftains they both follow. No wonder they fit so well together."

"MacNeil. It is a Scots name, as well," whispered Jamie from the *travois*. Mack leaned down to him. Jamie's lips were dry and pale, but his eyes were open. "The MacNeils also had chieftains and wore kilts. I think you must have a kilt next, Mack, since you have mastered long skirts and breeches." He winced and caught his breath in a sob of pain as John and Alex inadvertently jostled the him. John swore loudly at his clumsiness.

"Jamie," whispered Mack. "Lie still and do not talk." She lifted his hand to her cheek. Jamie could feel the tears on her cold skin.

"It is his leg that is broken, not his lips," Samuel corrected, in a effort to cheer them.

"How observant of you, Samuel." Jamie squeezed Mack's hand. "I do think I am fortunate that it was not worse. It all happens to me, doesn't it? I am sorry, John."

"Hush, now," John said gently. "It was a simple accident and we will heal you up in no time at all."

"Rest, Jamie. We will be at the Castle in just a short while," Samuel added.

They made their way through the forest. The sun dropped behind the trees and the wind fell. Falling snow hissed around them like a thousand white snakes. Owela went on ahead at a trot. It was almost certain that their approach had been noted, but he would call out and alert the watchers in the village that friends were coming to the Castle. Mack squinted as he disappeared into the snowfall. One second she could see him, and then he was gone. There was a sadness to it somehow. Mack felt herself shiver.

They plodded on, the snow becoming heavier as darkness crept in. Mack slipped and fell to her knees. Samuel pulled her to her feet. He did not release her, but held her arm so that she would not slip again.

Then there was a muffled sound in the distance. Drums. Like the beating of hearts, they pulsed in the night. Voices could be heard calling out, and the warm lights of torches made a yellow glow beyond the snowfall. Mack heard Owela's laughter, and then there he was in front of her, his hair dusted with snow, his eyes bright with happiness at the homecoming.

"The Castle is only a short way ahead, John. Let them help," he said. Two strong young men carefully took the stretcher from John and Alex, who flexed their stiff fingers gratefully. There were other men as well, and they all seemed to know John and Samuel. They called out greetings. Everyone, even John and Samuel, spoke Oneida, and so Mack had no idea of what was being said.

Out of the storm's whiteness appeared a dark wall. It was a building — one of many. People stood outside its entrance, their voices low and curious.

"Go carefully now," heeded John. "We must get this thing into a longhouse without dumping my brother on his head."

"I would appreciate that one small consideration," Jamie said, laughing feebly and gritting his teeth with the pain.

Suddenly they were in the village; the Oneida Castle lay before them. Huge longhouses loomed in the darkness. Large log cabins and many smaller buildings sat in the snow. People walked between the longhouses or stood in groups laughing and talking. Fires lit the darkness here and there. On an ordinary night everyone would usually be inside the buildings, but this night was different. It was the first heavy snow of winter, and children were racing about or rolling in the growing drifts and pelting each other with balls of snow.

And, more importantly, one of their own had come home. Mack saw hands reach out to touch or caress Owela as he passed by. She heard the words of welcome and hello. "*Sheko:li*, Owela!"

Dogs trotted up and down, sniffing at unfamiliar legs, their hackles rising, their paws leaving small prints as they went. Owela stopped in front of one longhouse. A woman waited there. It was his mother, Ní:ki. Owela walked to her, his face held carefully still, but his eyes were brimming with joy.

"*Sheko:li*, Mother," he said in Oneida. "Mam. It is so good to see you once more." He put his arms around his mother and held her as closely as he could.

"My son," she murmured.

Owela quickly explained what had befallen Jamie. Ní:ki looked concerned and hurried past him to lean over the stretcher. She examined Jamie's leg, then said something to Alex in rapid Oneida.

"We will take him to the small longhouse," she commanded in English. "There I can see to his leg and make certain that the bone is properly set, although I think that John will have done it well. It will be hurtful and the healing will take many weeks, but you will walk again. Come now." She motioned to the Oneida youths carrying Jamie to follow her and Alex. Mack started to go as well, but Owela stepped in her path.

"Jamie will be fine now," he assured her. "My mam will watch over him."

"I will go along and help her," Mack insisted. "I cannot just leave him." She tried to step around Owela.

"A moment," he said, his hand on her arm. "You will go there soon enough. For now you must all come with me to the longhouse where we meet. It would be a rude thing, indeed, not to pay your respects to my uncle." He led them among the longhouses and watching people.

"Your uncle?" Mack asked, as she and the others followed.

"He is my mother's brother and the *Sachem*, the Chief and a wise man," Owela explained. "He knows we are all here. Runners had brought word hours before, as we came through the forest."

"It is a sign of respect that we come before him, Mack," Samuel told her.

They stopped in front of another huge longhouse. Mack could smell wood smoke and the odor of cooking food. Her stomach rumbled and she realized how hungry she was.

Owela pushed back the deerskin flap that served as a door covering and led them in. It was a long building with a high arched ceiling. The light was poor but as they walked down the center of the structure, Mack's eyes became accustomed to the dimness. People sat around fires. Others stood against the longhouse's walls. Smoke rose toward small holes in the roof of the bark-covered building. It seemed that this must be some sort of gathering place, where perhaps the people came to greet visitors or make important decisions.

Mack coughed. Her eyes were beginning to water and sting a little with all the smoke. She squinted at John. He had reached into his hunting pouch and taken out something wrapped in soft leather. It was a wampum belt fringed with deerskin. It had been carefully woven of white shell beads. Dragonflies were worked down its length with beads the color of cobalt.

"It is a peace belt," John said in a low voice to Mack. He draped the belt over his forearm. "It signifies that we come here in friendship and goodwill."

A ring of Oneida men sat around the central fire. Except for the scalp locks that hung down their backs, their heads were smoothly shaved. Firelight glinted off of their silver earrings and the brass gorgets that hung around their necks. The men were all were heavily tattooed. Fragrant smoke rose from the pipes a few of them smoked, while they sat relaxed under the striped trade blankets draped across their shoulders. There was a muffled sound of low conversation and then silence. The man's voice that broke it was deep and rumbly.

"*Sheko:li*, Owela. You are home again, nephew. You have been on a great adventure, as I hear it," the *Sachem* said in his own language. The man was older than the others. His long scalp lock was streaked with gray, and his face was as weathered as the rocks in the hillsides that rose above the Castle.

"*Sheko:li*, Uncle. Yes, it was quite an adventure," Owela answered with a happy laugh.

"And *sheko:li*, Laya'tal ha," the *Sachem* went on, addressing John in the Oneida name that had once been given to him. The old man looked long and hard at the peace belt John wore on his arm. He smiled and gestured in welcome.

"Laya'tal ha. It means Painter. He who makes the pictures," Owela whispered to Mack in a low voice.

"You have brought some new people with you to the Castle this time. Who are they?" asked the *Sachem* curiously. "Sit and tell me." John stepped forward and then sat down cross-legged on the floor of packed dirt.

"*Sheko:li, Sachem*," he said in greeting. Owela leaned close to Mack and translated so that she could understand what was being said. "You know Samuel." The *Sachem* nodded briefly. "I am bringing home my brother, Jamie, and the girl, Mack, whom I have taken under my roof as my daughter. We were all returning to Fort Detroit when an accident befell my brother. His leg was broken in a fall, and I would ask that you grant us sanctuary until he is well enough for us to set out again."

The hooded eyes of the *Sachem* watched John for a moment and then looked over the people who stood before him. The Canadian Roy had visited this place with John MacNeil a few times. Everyone enjoyed his good humor and joking.

He then turned his gaze upon Mack, who held herself straight and calm. The *Sachem* paused for a moment. He was struck by the expression on Mack's face, which, while not being in the least defiant, showed a strength that seemed odd in one so young. Her eyes were the color of a bright blue bird the *Sachem* had seen once as a boy. He glanced at his nephew Owela and saw that the youth's intent gaze was fastened on the girl, as well. The *Sachem* smiled to himself just a little at this, and then he shifted his attention back to John.

"Of course, you will stay here," he said warmly. "We have missed your pictures. I think there will be many pictures this time, and perhaps many stories from both you and my nephew."

John glanced once at Owela. "Indeed, *Sachem*. Very many."

The *Sachem* motioned to the doorway. "See to your friends and your daughter, then. They are weary from the journey. There will be time enough for stories."

John got to his feet and the others did the same. He took Mack by the arm and followed Owela out of the longhouse with Samuel behind them. The Oneidas watched them go by with a little curiosity, but were otherwise indifferent. The *Sachem* had spoken his welcome, and so the outlanders would be here amongst the people for a time.

Mack's thoughts were confused. How odd it all was. "My daughter," John had called her. She barely knew what to think of being spoken of as such, and yet John's hand closed protectively about her upper arm was such a comfort.

"You are like a daughter to me," John said suddenly. He could read her face easily enough. "The Oneida people love the children they take in, exactly as they would their own blood. I knew the *Sachem* would understand how much you mean to me, my dear."

Then for some reason, Mack thought of Thomas. Ben Sparks said something once about selling them to Natives. If Thomas has been kidnapped and is sold to them, he would be well-loved, would he not? she asked herself. She truly hoped so. There would be time enough to sort out all these thoughts later. For now it was enough to know they were safe here.

The cold air felt refreshing upon her face and neck. Snowflakes fell thickly and their icy touch brushed her lips. There was no talk as Owela led them among the longhouses. Most of the people had gone inside. Only a few children remained out in the night, but even they were being dragged, protesting and whining, to their beds.

Owela stopped in front of a smaller longhouse. It had the same arched shape and bark-covered walls as the others, but it was shorter in length and, surprisingly, it had a door. Owela flipped the latch up, pushed the door open, and motioned them inside. Mack expected the same smoky haze to be hanging in the air, but although the longhouse was redolent with the smell of burning wood — and was that stew? — there was no more smoke in the air than there might have been in a frontier cabin.

"It is the 'small longhouse,' as we call it," Owela said, running his hands through his snow-dampened hair. "There are the big longhouses here and the smaller log buildings some families choose to live in. But this small longhouse is for visitors. They let my da build it years ago for the French and English and Scots who sometimes stayed. It was as much for us as for them, our ways being so different and all."

At the end of the structure was a small fireplace of river stones. Bright flames crackled. A glow from the coals rose and fell as the draft moved about them. An iron pot hung on a trammel. Something tempting bubbled and simmered within it. Mack's mouth watered and her stomach ached with hunger. There were two large cubicles on each side of the longhouse. In them were sleeping platforms. Blankets that might be dropped across the openings for privacy were neatly rolled across the tops of them.

Jamie lay in one of the cubicles near the hearth. His head was pillowed on several folded bearskins. Another covered his body. His broken leg was displayed. It was firmly held between the two stout branches and packed with moss, which peeped out from the soft deerskin in which it was bound. Ní:ki, who sat at his side, was spooning food into his mouth while Alex watched. Mack rushed forward.

"I will live, Mack," Jamie said weakly as he swallowed. "It hurt like the very devil when she checked it and packed it with moss, but she gave me a stick on which to bite. I fear I fainted again."

"You were a brave boy," said Ní:ki. "The stick was nearly bit in two before you cried out."

"Owela!" piped up a high voice in hurt tones. "You have not even said hello to me yet!"

A little girl of perhaps eight years sat on Jamie's other side. The child had black hair carefully braided in a smooth plait, and she held a doll in her arms. With her round face and snapping eyes, she was a tiny version of Ní:ki, who without doubt, must be her mother.

"I have not forgotten you," Owela said with affection. He scooped her up into his arms. "How could I forget my best sister, Sá:l? Has she been tormenting you, Jamie? She has a grand talent for it, does she not?"

"Your *only* sister," she laughed. Owela swung her in the air, then set her down. She threw her arms around his waist and then stared hard at Mack.

"You must not gawk at Owela's friends," scolded her mother. "They are guests here." The child's eyes dropped, then she looked up at Owela in mischief.

"The others I know, but who is the great tall one?" asked Sá:l. "You have forgotten the great tall woman. Will you tell me her name?"

"I did not forget. I think you and she will become fast friends," Owela told the child. "Mack, this is my only sister, Sá:l. You might call her Sarah, for that is what her name means in English, and she does love to hear it spoken as such. Sarah, my friend, Mack."

The little girl took Mack by the hand to lead her through the longhouse, showing her every corner and stick of furniture. Mack looked back apologetically at Jamie, but he smiled in understanding. He was quite comfortable, in spite of the pain. Sarah chattered away happily. Was this longhouse not remarkable? Did all the English have such odd things in their longhouses? Da and Owela had made the table and chairs themselves, and it was great fun to come here sometimes and sit on them with bowls of food set out on the table. Was Mack hungry? Then she must have stew in one of the wooden bowls stacked neatly on a shelf.

As Mack was shown around the longhouse, John and the others hung their damp blankets to dry near the fire. Then they all sat there to warm themselves as they ate.

Alex pulled a bottle of rum from a high shelf and poured out small cups of the strong liquid. "My father. Is he well?" he asked John.

"Wallace and Natka were both well when last I saw them. No one would dare to touch even an apple on the island while they are there," John laughed. He carried his cup to Jamie.

"Just a little," John cautioned, holding Jamie's head that he might take a sip. "It will help you to sleep."

"A little is more than enough," said Jamie grimacing, but then the rum reached his belly to spread its heat there. He gave a deep, tired sigh.

"There is no more to do for him at the moment," Ní:ki said softly. Jamie's eyes were closing. The food, the pain, and now the rum had worn him out. Mack herself was exhausted. She tried valiantly to stay awake and listen to the conversation of those settled near the fire.

"We must all go to our beds, I think," John decided for them. "Samuel, there are blankets and bearskin robes within the cubicle. Mack, Jamie may need something in the night. Can you sleep near him?" She nodded and glanced at Owela.

"I shall return to the longhouse of my clan," he said in answer to her silent question. His parents and sister already stood at the small longhouse's door. Ní:ki held Sarah's hand in her own.

Suddenly the child pulled away and scampered across the floor to the cubicle where Jamie lay sleeping. She carefully placed her doll across Jamie's chest. It was a simple toy made of a corn husk with arms and legs of the same braided stuff. Its hair was black wool, and it wore tiny pieces of clothing, a blouse, shawl, and skirt much like its owner's.

Mack looked down at the doll. "It has no face."

"No child's doll has a face here," explained Owela. He guided his sister back to their mother and father, who then left, shutting the door behind them. "There is an old tale of a vain cornhusk doll who spent all her days staring at her beauty in the reflection of a pool of still water. The Creator took away the reflection. Since then, the dolls of our children have no faces. It is the beauty inside that matters, you see. That and nothing else." He coughed to clear his throat, surprised at himself for telling her this. Why did he want to say so much about the Castle and his life here these days?

John sensed the awkward moment and spoke up. "It will be a busy time tomorrow with the visiting and feasting and all. Such things always take place when guests come to the Castle. You will surely meet the Three Sisters, Mack."

"Do you know of them?" Owela was asking her.

Mack shook her head at his question and lifted her shoulders. "Are they relations or friends? And whose sisters might they be?" Mack asked him.

Owela laughed out loud at this. "Why, they are the sisters of all the Oneidas. They are the corn, beans, and squash. We call them the Three Sisters. No longhouse feast would be without them, as you will see in time."

"My thanks for all your help, Owela," John said, as he poked the fire and set on another small log.

"It is my pleasure, John. Sleep well, now. You are safe in this place, for I will watch over you." Owela left the longhouse and disappeared into the falling snow. John closed the door behind him. Mack was not certain if he had been speaking to John or her, but she was far too tired to think about it.

"To your rest, Mack." John kissed her forehead. Then he climbed into the cubicle where Samuel was already settled. Mack heard them talking in low tones for a long while.

Mack crept in next to Jamie, taking care not to bump against him. His injured leg was on the opposite side, but still she did not wish to disturb his rest. When she lifted the blankets, she could feel his familiar warmth. She looked at the doll that lifted and fell with his even breathing. Its featureless face was turned toward her. This world is so different from mine, she thought.

CHAPTER FIFTEEN

Jamie's grumpy voice woke her the next morning. Someone had closed off the opening of their cubicle with the wool flap. A few tiny shafts of sunlight dropped down like white needles where the chinking of mud and moss had come loose a bit in the longhouse's walls. Other than the grumbling next to her, all was quiet within the longhouse.

"I have been sleeping on something. What is it? A doll. Why am I sleeping with a doll?" Jamie complained. Mack propped herself up on an elbow and regarded him. His eyes were puffy and his hair stood out wildly in all directions.

"Sarah left it for you last night after you had fallen asleep. I suspect she will be back to claim it and your company today," Mack said as she sat up.

John pulled aside the blanket. "You passed the night comfortably? We rose early. Samuel is out in the village, but I thought it would be best to let you two sleep. You will want the chamber pot, I suspect, Mack. There is one behind the screen in that corner. When you are finished,

I will bring it here to you, Jamie, and give you whatever help you need."

Mack got out of the cubicle and went behind the screen while Jamie felt around his person with growing horror. "Well, it seems someone has cut off my breeches, so that problem is solved," he said in a small voice. Mack roared with laughter, then clapped a hand over her mouth.

"It had to be done," John told him practically. "It would not have made sense to simply cut off one leg. When the time comes, we will provide you with a fine breechcloth and a warm set of leggings." There was more choked laughter from behind the screen.

Mack came out and handed the chamber pot to John. After helping Jamie, he came out of the cubicle and set the pot on the floor. "I will show you later where to empty this." He looked around. "There is a lavabo here somewhere, a big copper one that guests use for bathing sometimes," he suggested, knowing Mack's preferences. "Perhaps you may wish to warm water and bathe more thoroughly later, but when I am here I do as the others do."

Mack began to braid her hair. "And that is what?" she asked John.

"I do not wash at all." He grinned at the way Mack wrinkled her nose at the thought. She could go as long as necessary in an unwashed state — most did — but she preferred the feel of clean cloth against clean skin. "Or there is the sweat lodge."

"What, pray, might that be?" asked Mack. "Would you not feel even grimier all covered in sweat?"

"Not at all." John poured tea into cups for the three of them. "For the men here, the sweat lodge is often part of a cleansing ceremony. It cleanses both the body and the spirit. A new lodge is built of saplings each time. Water is sprinkled over hot stones that are carried to its center. There is a wonderful smell of cedar and greenness. Trust me, Mack, after a quarter hour within the lodge and a swim in the river or a roll in the snow, one might not be cleaner."

"I do think she will take your word for it, John," said Jamie. He was well awake now and in great pain from his leg. His forehead was damp with pearls of moisture, and his mouth was a thin, pale line. Mack watched him helplessly.

"*Sheko:li*," called Ní:ki from the longhouse's entrance. Owela, Sarah, and she came in. Ní:ki carried a covered iron pot from which wisps of steam were escaping. They all called back greetings to her. "I set this to brewing last night and it will be good and strong. You have pain?" She peered down at Jamie's drawn face.

"Some. A little. It hurts like mad!" he admitted.

Ní:ki fussed about, wiping his brow with a scrap of cloth and lifting the blanket to check his leg. "Well, this will give you relief. It is willow bark tea — a good strong batch. Foul tasting, but good for pain. A cup in the morning, one near midday, and another in the evening."

She dipped a large cup into the pot and set it out to cool so that Jamie would not burn his mouth. They placed more rolled blankets behind Jamie and helped him ease himself into a half-sitting position. When the willow bark tea had cooled, Ní:ki carefully passed the cup to him.

"I will float away if I have to drink three of these!" exclaimed Jamie. He sipped, grimaced, and slowly drank it all down. "Shall I sleep with the chamber pot in my arms?"

He passed the empty cup back to Ní:ki. Sarah had stood back, watching all of this, restrained only by Owela's hand on her shoulder. Now he released her and playfully ruffled her hair. She ignored this and headed straight for Jamie.

"You will want your doll back." He held it out to her. Sarah nodded her head, her long braid swinging across her back.

"Yes, I do need her badly," Sarah said happily. She took the doll in her arms. "She watches over me in the night, you see." Jamie's eyes grew wide at the thought of this.

"Does she have a name, this doll?" he asked her. Sarah climbed carefully onto the bedding and settled herself near him, away from his leg.

"She does, but she will not tell you, for it is unseemly to ask a person such a thing," she scolded, her nose in the air. Owela started to correct his sister for this, for how could Jamie know the ways of his people? But Mack touched his arm and he stopped.

"Well, then I shall ask you politely." Jamie persisted. "What is her name, if you might be so good to share it with me?"

John, smiling at this exchange between his brother

and the girl, turned to Mack. "Shall we go out into the village? Owela must show every bit of it to you."

"I will stay behind in case Jamie has a need of anything," offered Ní:ki.

Mack and John pulled matchcoats around themselves and put on their mittens. John took his musket from where it stood in a corner. With Owela leading them, they left Jamie to the talk of faceless dolls and went out into the morning.

The Castle was a sprawling village. Radiating from the road that ran through it were more than a dozen longhouses the Oneida men had built with long, flexible saplings. Slabs of elm bark chinked with mud and moss kept out the rain. In winter or in foul weather, skins were hung across the openings at each end to stop the wind. There were other long buildings of roughly squared logs, something halfway in appearance between the longhouses and the cabins built by outsiders.

More than one family lived in the bigger longhouses — there were as many as eighty people, Owela explained, all members of the same clan. The Oneida had three clans — the wolf, bear, and turtle. The women took care of the longhouse and all its possessions, and the eldest woman in the clan had the privilege of the cubicle nearest the doorway. The women had tremendous power within the clan and the Castle, Owela told them.

"They choose the Chiefs, you see. We all trace our lines through the blood of our mothers. It is not your father who matters in this, since the line passes down through the women."

"You have no surname, no last name?" asked Mack in surprise. She had thought him to be called Doig as his father was. "What would your children be called, then?"

Owela's brows drew together at the question, and he shook his head. "No. I have only the name that was given me. That and the wolf clan say who I am."

John could see her confusion. "We will be here all this winter, most likely. You will have time to understand something of Owela's people."

Mack became very quiet as they walked through the village. She recalled her thoughts of last night about how different the ways of the Oneida were from those of the English. Mack felt a strangeness beginning between them and, try as she might, she could not stop it. She listened to Owela talk on about the sweat lodge and the storage pits and the gardens. The burial platforms were there, too, it seemed. How odd to lay one's dead high above the earth rather than within it. The gulf widened a bit more.

Owela stopped at the doorway of one longhouse. Mack recognized it as the place where he had greeted his parents the night before. He held back the flap of deerskin that covered the opening, and, stooping, they all went into the dim building.

There were partitions on each side. Some were empty. Blankets and robes of fur were folded or piled within them. From other cubicles faces peered. People leaned out on their elbows, watching with open curiosity as the procession passed down the length of the longhouse. A child ran by, and then another, toward the fallen snow outside.

Mack looked up. Corn and tobacco hung above their heads. Baskets, pots, and rolls of belongings rested in an upper layer of cubicles to each side. All down the length of the longhouse, low fires burned with pots of food hanging suspended above them.

Every few steps someone would stop them, a warrior who would clap Owela across the shoulders and welcome him home just one more time, or an elder who would call out for news of a mutual friend who lived in a far-off place. The women exclaimed over Mack's clothing and her great height. Children ran their hands along her breeches and felt the linings of her shoe-paks. The building smelled of the dozens of people who lived inside it, wood smoke, and cooking food.

And when Mack picked up a baby and took him from his mother to coo over the small, dear face, the infant clenched both hands in her hair and pulled the leather tie from the end of her braid. Try as she might, Mack could not coax the baby to give back the thong. Fearing that the child would begin to wail, she left her thong behind. She looked back one time to see the baby waving the tie about his face like a tiny trophy of war.

At last they exited the longhouse and stood outside for a while. Mack breathed in great lungfuls of the cold, fresh air. She ran her fingers through her hair, loosening the last of the braid and shaking it down to her shoulders in dark ripples so that the breeze would not blow it across her eyes. Voices called to them. They turned to see Samuel and some of the Oneida men coming toward them. They had been out in the forest, and they all carried rabbits and squirrels.

"It has been good hunting, I see," John called back. Samuel waved a squirrel above his head.

"The pots of the small longhouse will be very full tonight," Mack laughed when the party of triumphant hunters surrounded them.

"It is not only for the small longhouse," Owela corrected gently. "Some will go there, but the rest will come to our longhouse, and something will be saved for those who have not had such luck this day." Mack felt a flush creeping up her neck to think of how selfish her words must have sounded to him. Here, it seemed, they shared everything.

"Oh, she is very aware of that," Samuel said brightly. "She only means that she can barely wait to set herself to skinning a plump squirrel for our dinner."

Mack's eyes widened in dread, but she quickly recovered. "Yes. That is precisely what I meant. I can barely restrain myself. In fact, it is my favorite task second only to emptying a chamber pot."

"Then you may carry this fat fellow back to the small longhouse," Samuel laughed and he thrust a limp squirrel under Mack's nose. John's hand flew out and he scooped up the animal.

"I will take this for you, Mack." He squinted up at the sun, judging the time. "It is near midday and they will be preparing to dose Jamie. Perhaps we should go back to the small longhouse, Samuel, and rescue him from Sarah. After all, he has been at her mercies all morning." John turned to follow the others, who had already started out. "Why don't you take Mack beyond the village, Owela, to show her what she could not see in the darkness last night? It is quite lovely out there today, I would think."

Mack walked with Owela. Behind her she could hear the excited sounds of the men making their afternoon plans. Then they faded. The day was brilliant. Mack squinted at the openness and whiteness of the land surrounding the Castle. In the distance, heavily treed hills sloped up all about them. The flat fields that the Oneida people farmed were like a white trackless sea of snow. She felt a sudden change within herself, a sense of prickling discomfort, an odd sensation that had not once come upon her in all the times she had walked through the wilderness.

Mack looked at Owela, who was already heading out, pointing to this field and that one. He seemed so happy as he talked about how wonderful it all looked in the summer, with the trees so green and the corn standing tall in the fields. And in the autumn. How beautiful the oaks were then, gold and bronze with the sunlight on them. Then she understood. It was she who was the stranger in this place.

"There is so much to show you here, Mack. So much to tell you," he said suddenly.

Just then a cloud moved in and it began to snow again. Mack turned and looked back at the Castle. She had not ever seen anything like it in her life. There it crouched, the gray buildings made ghostly by the falling snow. She could hear the muffled sounds of everyday life coming from within, but out here, all was silent. There was only the soft sound that snow makes when it falls.

"It is wonderful," said Mack. "Your home is a beautiful place, Owela. I understand why you wished to come back to it."

"It will be your home as well." He faced the Castle as he spoke. "At least for a while, until Jamie is able to travel once more and you leave for John's island."

"Yes. For a while." A gust rose and snow swirled in small whirlwinds. As the snow hit her, tears came to Mack's eyes in an unwelcomed rush, and she angrily scrubbed a mitten across her face.

"The wind is strengthening," said Owela. He stared straight ahead and blinked hard several times. "It does make the eyes water. Let us go in." She followed him back to the village.

The weeks passed uneventfully, each day much the same as the other. Sometimes there were storms, hard, cruel bursts of shrieking weather that rattled the trees. Other times, it was sunny, and now and again even mild for the winters in this land. Jamie's leg healed more quickly than was expected. The pain was replaced with a deep itching that Ní:ki proclaimed was the sign of a knitting bone. They all took turns sitting with him, giving him simple tasks to do or telling him stories.

One afternoon Mack entered the small longhouse. She had forgotten the pouch that she always had tied around her waist. A fire snapped in the hearth. The room was quiet except for the sound of Sarah's high voice. She was telling a story to Jamie.

"There was, once upon a time, a warrior who married for his second wife the proudest woman that ever was known in the Castle. Her husband had died in the war between the English and the French and she had two daughters, who were exactly like her in every way. I think they were not kind girls, Jamie. You would not like them at all. The warrior had himself a young daughter. She was sweet and obedient and good. Like me!"

Mack crossed the room and sat down at the edge of the cubicle. She stroked back the hair that had escaped Sarah's braid. "Wherever did you hear this story, Sarah?" she asked in amazement.

"From Owela," Sarah answered happily. "He has told it to me every night since he has returned."

◇ ◇

There was always work to be done. The men went out to hunt each morning; now and again they were gone for a few days, camping out in the wintry forest. Mack did not worry. The woodcraft of Owela and the others was born of a knowledge handed down through timeless generations. Clenching her teeth, Mack learned to skin rabbits and pluck grouse. There was corn to parch or grind and fresh skins to scrape and prepare for tanning with the brains of the animals. At night, when she rolled herself in her blanket next to Jamie in their cubicle, Mack was exhausted but strangely content.

Slowly, a sense of excitement began to build within the Castle. The seven tiny stars were now high in the night sky. A midwinter festival would begin in a few days.

"It is nearly the end of January by my reckoning," John told Mack one night as they stared up into the sky. He pointed to the stars. "But the Oneida consider it to be midwinter when they can see those seven stars. They are the Pleiades and there is Orion."

Everyone talked of nothing else. Mack shivered to hear the women say that there was so much work to do. She now had some small sense of the Oneida tongue, for Owela and Sarah had been teaching her and Jamie words and phrases in the evenings. How could a person do more? She took a deep breath, squared her shoulders, and resolved to do no less than any other.

Two days later she sat in the meeting longhouse with dozens of other women from Owela's clan. For hours they had been stripping corn from the cobs for the soup they would cook that night. The festival would begin tomorrow and the soup must be ready. Jamie lay nearby on a pallet with Ní:ki and Sarah on either side of him. A great bundle of corn dropped in front of Mack. Owela stood near her, dusting off his hands. Behind him was John. Samuel and Alex Doig leaned against their muskets with only a casual interest in the work that was being done around them.

"You might help," Mack murmured grouchily to Owela. He raised his brows and looked down at her. There she sat, tangles of hair hanging around her face, her fingers red from twisting the corn cobs. He opened his mouth to say that this was women's work, and then for some reason he would never understand, he did not. Instead, he dropped down beside her and picked up an ear of corn.

"Excellent choice, Owela!" John laughed. "You at least stand a chance."

Jamie shifted slightly and took the bait. "A chance at what, John?"

"Why, the prize, you see. I first learned of this when I was a young man traveling in the colonies. There they have a thing that they call a husking bee. It is an exciting event. Everyone — the women and men — husk the corn, and as they work they search for something. The person who finds that object wins the prize. I thought it might be interesting if we did the same here today."

Samuel shrugged his shoulders. "What is it they must find, John?"

John looked around, an innocent expression on his face. "What must they find? They must find the tiny cob of red corn that is hidden in the pile. It is a simple enough task."

"Simple indeed, John, but it does not seem like much of a prize to me," Samuel observed doubtfully.

"I do not think I would husk or shuck corn for the joy of owning a red cob," commented Alex under his breath. "They do have strange ways outside of the Castle. But it is cruel to laugh at their expense, I suppose."

"No, no! The cob of red corn is not the prize. It is simply that the person who finds the cob has the right to claim a kiss from the one of their choice," John told them patiently. The circle of people grew still. Mack could feel Owela's eyes on her but she did not return his stare.

There was not a sound for an instant, and then Samuel

roared, “Let the contest begin!” as he fairly dove into the corn.

John passed ears of corn to Jamie, who stripped the corn from the cob as fast as he could. Laughter and shouting echoed through the longhouse, until others came to stare and chuckle over the strange sight. Husks flew like bits of pale feathers. Piles of cleaned cobs mounted high and the baskets filled with rivers of fat golden kernels. Then it was over.

Alex stood and planted his hands on his hips. “Is this a cruel jest, John?” he asked, his voice gruff and his brows drawn down in pretended anger. Sarah giggled at her father. Mack rose to her feet and brushed the back of her hand across her damp forehead.

“It is no jest, Da,” Owela spoke up. “I found it nearly at once, but you were all working so well, I did think to let you finish your task.”

He held out his hand. In his palm was the small cob of corn, its red kernels the color of rubies. People surged around him to see it and Mack stepped back into the crowd. Owela stood up, looking past their heads, his eyes searching.

“Mack is missing the fun,” sighed Sarah, dusting off her bottom. “Wherever has she gone?”

◇ ◇

The next morning Owela came to the small longhouse. He did not mention the cob of red corn and neither did Mack. It seemed everyone else had forgotten, as well. There was only one thing that mattered — the festival had begun.

All day long the ceremonies and celebrations went on. The beating of drums and the singing could be heard, a brooding mysterious sound in the still air. People hurried back and forth from one longhouse to another. Men emerged from the sweat lodges, dripping with perspiration, their eyes clear and faces bright with the secret of what had happened within.

Many of the ceremonies were closed to Mack and any other who was not Oneida. She did not ask about these things. Some instinct warned that to do so would be the worst breech of etiquette in a world she was only beginning to understand. Still, there were some things she and the other outsiders could attend.

A game had begun in the fields outside the village that morning and had been running on for hours. There were two teams of fifty or so men. They all held sticks with scoops on the ends, scoops that looked like curved snowshoes. Back and forth they ran, trying to capture a leather ball and fling it across some point at either end of the long playing field. The snow became trampled and muddy. Men slid in the muck, elbows and knees skinned, slush dripping from their bodies. With each grand collision, the watching crowd groaned and cheered. It was *lacrosse*, Samuel explained, using the French word for the game.

"It is called *ga-lahs*, in Oneida," Owela added. "We have always played it."

Samuel grinned and slapped Owela across the shoulders. "Yes, and we Canadians, in our great wisdom, now play it as well."

"When does a game end?" wondered Mack.

"When one side drops down and cannot lift their sticks or run another minute," John laughed.

Children wandered onto the playing field and frantic mothers raced out to snatch them back. A pack of dogs ran alongside the players, nipping at heels and chasing their own tails. At one point the game was stopped when a dog stole the ball and had to be pursued into the woods. Panting, tongue lolling, it sat on the sidelines near the little boy who owned it to watch the rest of the game.

That night they walked to the meeting longhouse. John and Mack carried a kettle of corn soup between them. They also each carried another pot with some tasty food steaming within. There was baked acorn squash and a pudding of ground corn and maple sugar from last spring. Stews of muskrat, squirrel, and venison made the mouth water. It would all be shared amongst the people of each clan. They dipped their fingers or bowls into the pots to serve themselves and groaned over how good it was.

"Are you hungry, my friend?" Owela asked Jamie, as he carried him in his arms through the night to the gathering. The boy's leg might be healing, but he could walk no distance safely on his own.

"I am half-starved," he exclaimed. They reached the longhouse and Owela carefully set Jamie down by the fire near Mack.

It was a long, noisy evening. There was drumming, dancing, and the Oneida songs that echoed through the longhouse. Owela and his family joined them to sit and laugh and talk and tell stories.

Mack would always remember the stories from that night. Not only did they have to be told at least ten times, it seemed, the tales also had to be acted out. The crowd sat hushed as the mountain lion poised to attack — John made a fine lion, growling in his most fierce fashion — until the children hid their faces. When brave Owela rescued Mack and Jamie, the young women sighed and closed their eyes. And the story of the tea party was told again and again, with Mack and Owela tossing invisible bales of tea into Boston's harbor as the people cheered.

"You were correct," Mack said as she pretended to toss another bale. "If it will be said for all time that Iroquois had done the deed, how perfect it is that you were there, Owela."

Owela nodded and leaned close to her as he picked up an invisible bale. "Secretly though, so as to not give offence," he whispered, "I must tell you that only the British might think to start a war over dried plants."

The story finished. They both sat down near the fire.

"Well done!" Jamie cried. "I only wish I could have helped you. What memories that brought back!"

Then the longhouse began to grow quiet. Mack saw that everyone was watching the *Sachem*. He looked around at his people and their guests. Then he himself told a story and the longhouse was silent as he spoke. "Long ago, when we built our first village, a great stone appeared that was unlike anything the people had ever seen. Even when the village was moved, the stone followed us. We took our name from this stone." There were murmurs of agreement.

Owela looked carefully at Mack before speaking. "It is true. We believe that this happened, you see. We are the People of the Standing Stone, the Oneida."

Mack looked back at him and nodded slightly. "It is a strange tale," she said softly. "I do not understand it, but I understand how much your home and your people mean to you."

"The feast will go on all night and then begin again at dawn," Owela said, suddenly turning from her. "Join us in the game of *ga-lahs* tomorrow, John. You and Samuel on one side and myself and my da on the other. We will battle it out. What say you?"

For some reason this made Mack's skin creep. She had almost been comfortable tonight, as though the first small beginnings of belonging here might be possible. Owela's words, as innocent as they were, turned this notion to smoke. The feeling of a great difference between the two of them made her nearly ache inside.

"A fine idea, my friend. Prepare to be crushed."

The festival went on and on for many more days until no one could stand it any more. Then it was time to settle into the ordinary routine of winter once again. Almost as though the weather knew how it must behave, an icy cold gripped the Castle and storms returned.

CHAPTER SIXTEEN

"My, those are colorful words you are using," Mack observed. She bit her lip hard to keep from smiling and glanced at Owela. "I can only imagine who taught you the Oneida versions." Jamie was limping around the longhouse, swearing mightily in English and Oneida at the pain in his leg and the weakness he felt after nearly six weeks of inactivity.

Owela kept an innocent expression on his face. Although the bone of Jamie's thigh was healing, and each day he walked with a bit more strength, he still could not have gone far in the deep snow that now lay all around the Castle. "Be patient with yourself, Jamie. How could you manage snowshoes? Even bare ground will be a challenge until your muscles are stronger."

"I am not a patient person," Jamie grumbled. He sat down in a chair by the fire. "But I am a gentlemen and so I will curse as quietly as I can. But I have been rendered nearly insane with this!"

Mack knew this was close to being true. It was a slow, monotonous time and there were only the endless household tasks to keep her busy. "Here. I will let you help me mend this stocking. You are becoming very good at sewing, you know. Why, you might be able to open a shop when we return to the island." Mack pretended to be cheerful, but she was also restless at being cooped up in the small longhouse.

When the storms passed, John and Samuel led Jamie outside for short walks. John would wander off on his own to draw the countryside and the occasional bird or animal. In the evenings they would all exclaim over the pictures. Sometimes John drew one or another of them by firelight. Sarah especially loved to see her face appear on the papers.

Mack and Owela often left the Castle to wander up into the hills. He showed her where he had played and hunted as a boy, where a bear slept beneath a huge windfall, its breath rising through the snow in a thin mist, and where wolves had made a kill of an old deer, its bones now picked clean by scavengers.

One afternoon as they walked out together, Owela bent suddenly and picked up a handful of the deep snow. He packed it into a ball and threw it as hard as he could. "You have been here at the Castle all the winter," he said in an off-handed fashion. He stopped and gestured with a mittened hand toward the village. "How does this place seem to you now?"

The Castle stood there below them. Mack looked down at it, considering her answer carefully. It had once appeared very strange to her, but now Mack saw it in a different way. Owela waited beside her, his breath rising in a cloud around his face.

"I truly like it here, Owela. Your people have been so good to us, and the land is so lovely," Mack began. Then she stopped. "You know it is not my home, Owela. It is yours and I could not live here, I think." She threw up her hands and laughed helplessly. There was no humor in the sound. "Not here, nor England, and maybe not even on John's island. Would that not be rich, after all we have done to return? It would be just my poor luck to no longer feel so at home there. Perhaps I shall wander forever!"

"I do understand," Owela told her as lightly as he could. His voice had lost some of its warmth. "I know nothing of England, but I do know I could not ever make my home in a place like Boston."

And so there it was. It had all been spoken and there was not another thing to say.

Less snow fell. One day the sun rose warm and bright to melt the icicles into dripping streams. Patches of dead grass appeared here and there in the fields as the drifts of snow shrank. Someone said she had seen a robin. Another mentioned that he had heard a flock of grackles in the forest, their cries grating like rusty metal.

One afternoon John stood in the open doorway of the longhouse. "You know," he mused. He took a deep breath of the air and nodded to himself. Mack stepped out near him and set down the bucket she meant to fill with water.

"What is it I must know?" she asked, putting her arm around his waist in affection. He squeezed her shoulder in return.

"That it will not be so long until we are back at Fort Detroit. I think spring has come at last, and we must make our plans to leave," John announced.

Mack should have been happy. Excitement should have filled her at the thought of leaving the Castle and returning to John's house once again. It was there, but beneath it all was a sad feeling she could not explain.

They made their plans carefully. It had to be Fort Niagara first. The going would be very slow to save Jamie's leg. By the time they arrived there, any last snow would be gone, and the lakes and rivers would be open for canoes. Word spread through the Castle as quickly as tiny green buds spreading their pale lace across the forest. The strangers would leave soon, but then they were not really strangers now, were they? Mack heard the talk. She had enough Oneida now after all these weeks, and this friendly acceptance warmed her.

They packed their few possessions and slowly set the small longhouse in order. It almost looks as though we have not ever been here, thought Mack. No moccasins lay kicked off in a corner. Packs and bedrolls rested by the door near the weapons that would be carried home. Canteens were filled and supplies of parched and dried corn, beans, and rice were ready.

"We must say our goodbyes in the same fashion as we made our hellos," John decided the evening before they left.

They walked through the village, taking a route they all knew well by now. People who had ignored them months ago now smiled, or gestured, or waved in greeting as they passed by. There was the big meeting longhouse. It had been patched and chinked again to repair the damage done by the winter weather. Each of them stooping, they entered the lodge one by one and followed John to its center. Owela and his family were there, standing behind the *Sachem*. Men sat around the fires watching quietly.

The old *Sachem* looked up calmly at their approach and motioned that John sit beside him. He looked over the visitors just as he had done the first time he had seen them. Smoke from the pipe he held drifted into the air.

"You will leave us, Laya'tal ha." The *Sachem* nodded to himself. "You have enough provisions and ammunition? You must tell me if you lack anything. All we have is yours."

John dropped his eyes, touched by the *Sachem*'s generosity. "We have all we need, *Sachem*. Indeed, we leave here far richer than when we came. What we take with us cannot be seen, for it is a gift of the heart. You have been good to us, and for my companions, I thank you." John slipped his document case from his shoulder and pulled out a rolled paper tied with leather. "I hope to show my thanks to you with this, *Sachem*."

The *Sachem* nodded his head and took the roll. Slowly, he untied the leather thong and unrolled the paper. At first his face was unreadable. Then deep lines creased his weathered skin and he smiled in pleasure.

Owela looked down. On the paper was a drawing of the Castle. John had sketched the longhouses and buildings from the hillside. There was the small longhouse with smoke drifting from its chimney and two people — a man and a woman — standing outside it.

The *Sachem* inclined his head, accepting John's gift. Carefully he rolled the drawing, set it aside, and drew deeply on his pipe. He let the smoke escape in a thin stream that rose and mingled with the smoke of the longhouse's fires. Then he passed the pipe to John, who did the same thing.

"It was a pleasure to have you among us, Laya'tal ha. Not all the French and English are such good guests, you know." The *Sachem* wrinkled his brow thoughtfully. "You hunted and brought food to the cook pots, and your daughter worked alongside our women each day. You respected our ways, not asking rude questions, or coming uninvited to the ceremonies that are for the Oneida people alone. You must return some time, my friend."

"I shall," John told him honestly. "I cannot speak for the others, though. It is a long, hard voyage from Detroit."

The *Sachem* glanced at Mack, who waited in silence, her eyes respectfully lowered. Feeling his gaze upon her, Mack raised her face and for a moment her eyes met those of the old man. It almost seemed as though he could see into her heart, her very mind, so closely did he regard her, and then his mouth twitched in a smile and he turned back to John.

"Perhaps we shall see one or another of your kin again," the *Sachem* predicted. "Who can say what may happen between people in time? Journey safely, Laya'tal ha."

John led them from the fire. Owela and his family followed behind them. They all walked to the small longhouse in silence.

"We will be here to see you off in the morning," Alex announced briskly, "but we shall say our goodbyes now this night. Fare thee well, John MacNeil. May your journey be a good one, and may you come across not a single mountain lion. And greet my father and Natka warmly for me when you see them again."

Mack was grateful for his light, teasing words. The thought of leaving was not a happy one; losing the friendships she had made was very painful. The men thumped each other's backs heartily and clasped hands. John made promises to return next year. Perhaps Alex might journey to Pêche Island that fall and go farther north to trap. Who could tell? Hearing the cheery plans, Mack felt her throat tighten.

Only Owela hung back a bit. "I do not care for farewells," he told them as he grasped John's hand and squeezed Samuel's shoulder. His eyes brushed each of the people with whom he had spent so much time. "And so I will not say them. Jamie, take care not to fall from any cliffs on the way home. All of you keep your eyes upon him." Then he turned to Mack. He opened his mouth to say something, paused, and then began again. "Be well, Mack."

"Be well, Owela. You are a true and dear friend to me." Somehow this was both too much to say and yet not enough. You saved our lives, she wanted to tell him. I have learned so very much from you about this land and your people, and I cannot possibly believe that our friendship ends here. But she only smiled and said again softly, "Be well." With his family around him, Owela walked away to their longhouse.

"There we are, then," said John heartily. "To your beds and have a sound sleep. Dawn will come early."

"It always does," Jamie commented to Samuel. "Why would he say so?"

"Do not ask such questions of the rapier-like MacNeil powers of observation, my friend," corrected Samuel.

They said their goodnights and climbed into their beds. Mack could hear quiet conversation for a few minutes, and then only light snores and breathing. She knew Jamie lay awake beside her and nearly turned to him to say something, but then she did not really feel like talking. She lay there for a long while, positive that she would not sleep at all, finally closing her eyes in hope that she might. When Mack opened them again, it was morning.

"It will be a fine day, perfect for a long walk," John was saying.

Mack crawled from her bed. She was tired and she had a most uncomfortable crick in her neck. She rubbed it hard to ease out the stiffness. The others sensed her mood and left her to herself as they prepared to leave. Only Jamie reached out and squeezed her hand once.

"Check carefully to make certain you have all you wish to bring with you," John cautioned. "We cannot turn back. Are we ready?" There were nods all around. He opened the door and stepped outside.

Past John's shoulder Mack could see the dawn sky rich with color. Ripples of birdsong rose in the forest beyond the village. She, too, stepped out into the morning and then stopped. A crowd of people waited, all quiet. Alex, Ní:ki, and Sarah stood in front. Behind them, hundreds stood still, children peeking shyly from behind their mothers' skirts, young girls with laughing faces, and warriors serious and watchful. Old people leaned against each other, their eyes bright with interest.

Then in Oneida someone called, "Goodbye, Laya'tal ha! Goodbye, Mack," and it began. Farewells and good wishes rang into the morning. People began to sing a song for a good journey, and children ran about wildly as the dogs barked and growled and raced around them.

"You could not just leave," laughed Alex. "Such a thing does not happen here."

"Not without a proper send-off, it seems," John agreed as someone slapped him across the shoulder and wished him good hunting on his way.

"Jamie! Jamie!" shrieked Sarah. "You must take this." She thrust her precious cornhusk doll into his hands. "She will watch over you in the night the same way she has always done for me."

Jamie knew enough of the Oneida ways now to understand that he could not even think to refuse such a gift, particularly one so personal as this. "We will look after each other," he said firmly, and he slipped the doll inside his pack. Sarah took his hand and walked alongside him until they were at the edge of the village. The crowd grew quiet and people stepped aside.

There was Owela. He reached inside his shirt and pulled out something. At first, Mack thought it was the locket, for his hand hid the object. Then he opened his palm and the small red ear of corn dropped onto his chest. Owela closed the distance between Mack and himself in a few quick steps.

"I have not yet claimed my prize," he said quietly.

"No, you did not," she answered him.

Owela reached out and took her hands. He wanted to pull her to him, but he did not dare to do so, for fear of what she might say. Mack would have thrown her arms around his neck, but she was sure that she might never have been able to let go. Owela kissed her once on the mouth, their hands clasped between them.

"I thought he would never get around to it," Jamie whispered to John.

Then it was over. Mack pulled back her hands and Owela stepped away.

"Come, my dear," said John gently, putting his arm around Mack's shoulder. "Let us go." She nodded and followed him in silence. Suddenly she stopped and turned around. Owela stood there, as if he was carved of stone, holding the corn cob in his hand.

"It was you who did it, was it not?" she called to him. He shook his head slightly, not knowing what she meant. "The dragonfly in the cave. It was your dream and your painting."

Owela did not answer, but Mack saw one corner of his mouth lift in a small smile and the look in his eyes told her the truth. She smiled back, then she turned around quickly and followed John and the others. Owela watched them until they disappeared in the forest.

The crowd slowly drifted away and then Owela was left alone. He held the red corn cob tightly, until he felt the pain in his hand. He opened his palm and saw that he had crushed the thing. Bits of corn lay loose in his hand. His face expressionless, he shook them off and, turning on his heel, walked away quickly, leaving the kernels of corn to lie there as bright as new blood. Later, a chipmunk came and took them all to its nest.

CHAPTER SEVENTEEN

"It is the strangest feeling," Mack said slowly. They had stopped for a moment. She took a deep breath of damp, lake-scented air as she looked curiously at a place she had not seen in nearly half a year. "It is almost like going back in time. It does not seem real to me somehow, John." Mack stared at Fort Niagara. There was the entrance, solid and secure with England's flag floating in the gentle breeze.

"I know precisely what you mean," John agreed. They all began to walk again. "It is always the same for me when I come in from the forests to a place where people have truly made their mark."

"Well, it will seem real enough when you get inside and have a bed to sleep upon," teased Jamie. There was a great deal of groaning and laughter from Mack. Even the hard sleeping platforms of the small longhouse were preferable to the ground on which they had slept these last weeks. The small longhouse. The Castle. Mack would not think of them.

They passed though the Gate of Five Nations and

entered the fort's enclosure. An officer stood in the open, grassy area beyond the entrance, in conversation with two young captains. The officer was Lieutenant Colonel Francis Smith. He looked very smart and elegant, every button polished, a wig set perfectly upon his head, the very picture of what the military represented here in this country. His eyes crinkled and a wide grin split his face when he saw who was approaching.

"My word! I had news you were coming, but I can scarcely believe what I am seeing. Miss MacNeil, young Master MacNeil, you have led everyone on a merry chase, as I have heard it. Lord MacNeil, sir, it is good to see you and your family once again."

"Lieutenant Colonel Smith! I can say with honesty that we are most happy to be back here," John answered.

"Enough of this, now," Smith said briskly. "You must come into the stone house and refresh yourselves. Miss MacNeil, there is hot water and clean toweling at your disposal." Mack sighed inwardly with pleasure at the thought of such luxury.

"You are kind, sir," she thanked him, and they slowly crossed the grounds of the fort. There were many people here today going to the trade room at the stone house. Soldiers strode about in groups. Below them, the Niagara River churned and poured itself into Lake Ontario.

John and Lieutenant Colonel Smith walked a little ahead, talking quietly. The captains followed them. Then, suddenly, there was a screeching that nearly drowned out the muted sounds of their conversation. It was the squealing and laughter of a young child. As Mack was thinking that she had never heard such a happy, free sound in all her life, little Thomas came hurtling around the corner of the stone house in pursuit of a dog. He crashed directly into Mack with a great thump. She gasped in surprise, held him away from herself, and then hugged him closely.

"Thomas! However have you come here? What happened to you?" Mack looked from John, to the captains, back to Thomas.

Thomas was clinging to Mack as tightly as he could. "Miss Mack!" was all he could say, over and over, as he wept.

"You are safe now, Thomas," she soothed, stroking his hair. "Were you hurt? Did you run away?"

"No, he did not run away, but I do believe that I wish he would!" grumbled a deep voice. "He is far more trouble than his size would indicate." A familiar man stood in the doorway of the trade room.

"Elias Stack!" Jamie cried and he ran clumsily to Elias, who clapped both hands on Jamie's shoulders and assessed him carefully.

"Yes, it is me. You look well and fit enough, Jamie, my boy, although you must tell me what has happened to make you limp," Elias said in concern. He hugged Jamie hard. "Well, you do have some color in your cheeks at last. I had despaired of you for a while, there." Elias turned to Mack with a grin on his face. "And Miss Mack! Still in breeches, I see," he teased.

"Elias, how wonderful to see you," said Mack.

"Although if you tell me Molly Ladle is in there hiding and waiting to spring out at us, I shall faint."

Elias laughed aloud, the sound as rich and hearty as she remembered it. "You faint, Miss Mack? I surely think not. No, no. Molly Ladle is with the army to the east as she should be. Only I am here with this ragamuffin."

"How ever did you find him?" Mack wondered.

"It is a long, interesting story," Elias answered simply.

Smith broke in. "To the stone house with her first, Stack," he said. "Then food and whatever else they may wish. I will await you all in my quarters, Lord MacNeil."

Hugging Thomas one last time, Mack followed the two captains into the building. John, Jamie, and Samuel were behind her.

"Lord MacNeil, you and your brother are welcome to my room, sir," one captain piped up.

"And you to mine, Miss MacNeil, for as long as you wish to stay," the other added.

"My thanks, sir." Mack glanced at Samuel. The invitation had not been extended to him. She felt British civilization prick her with irritation. Back at the Castle all would have sat round the same fire. There it was again. The Castle. She put it out of her head and asked, "Samuel, where will you sleep?"

Samuel opened his mouth to answer. Something about the set of his shoulders and the muscle that jumped in his cheek told her that he was about to make his excuses and leave. But John put his hand on Samuel's arm and Samuel said nothing. John looked over at the officers, one eyebrow raised, a cool, questioning expression on his face. No insult had been made to his friend and none would be.

"And you as well, my good fellow," the first captain loudly offered. "Why, we cannot forget a friend of Lord MacNeil's, can we?"

Jamie elbowed Samuel. "You are most generous, monsieurs," Samuel answered, dodging the elbow as it came at him again. Then, climbing up the stairs to the second floor, he whispered, "I will pay you back nicely for that with horrible tortures, my friend. How long can you keep your head above water, Jamie?"

It was a warm day for April, and so John, Samuel, and Jamie decided to walk to the lake to swim. That would be bath enough. But for Mack, there was hot water and soap. Later, fed and rested, they, Elias Stack, and Thomas sat with Smith in his chambers. The officer poured spirits into glasses for them as they told him their story.

"You were wise to leave when you did, sir. Parliament did, indeed, close Boston's harbor. It shall remain closed until the taxes are paid on the tea the revolutionaries dumped in the harbor. As I said to you those months ago, they are nothing more than a pack of animals."

"Yes. Quite," said John with a small smile, glancing at Mack and Jamie briefly. Neither of them could look back at him, nor could they look at each other. Jamie carefully regarded the ceiling so that he would not burst into laughter.

"Yours is positively the most amazing tale I have heard in years, Miss MacNeil and Master Jamie," Smith went on. "Not simply the tale itself, but the shape of it. Your adventure was almost like a puzzle with all the pieces fitting together so neatly."

Mack swirled the Madeira around in her goblet, then took a tiny sip. She had barely lowered its level. "I have come to discover that sometimes things happen because they are meant to." She turned to Elias, who had said little to this point. "Which brings it all back to you, Elias. Surely it is no coincidence that you are here with Thomas, is it?" She stroked the child's hair as he sat on the floor, leaning his head against her leg.

Elias drank deeply from his cup. "No, it is not. I was traveling from German Flats to Albany and had been out for several days. There I was in my encampment, just sitting down to my evening meal, when I heard the sound of people approaching." Elias leaned comfortably back in his chair and settled to the tale. "I armed myself, for I was certain I would have the bad luck to have the strangers come upon me." He stopped and looked at each one of them.

"And did they?" Samuel urged him to continue.

"Indeed, they did," Elias went on slowly. "And although I have seen many distasteful sights in my life, I will say that only once before have I encountered a worse-stinking, more foul-mouthed ruffian. I knew him at once, although in the darkness he did not remember me, it seemed." Mack felt the hair at the back of her neck lift as Elias spoke. "Privy scum. But foul or not, I had little choice but to offer what small hospitality I could, since I am a gentleman at heart, as you so well know, Miss Mack. Besides, there was his companion to consider."

"Companion?" asked Jamie, who could barely stand the leisurely pace of the man's story.

"Me!" shrieked Thomas, jumping up. "Ben Sparks kidnapped me when I was out trying to find the last of those papers that told all about you, Miss Mack. He said what a fine prize I was, and that if he could not have you, then he would take me. He wanted to hurt you any way he might, I am certain of that. I bit him again and he struck me very hard. Then he made me watch while you and Jamie and everyone left the ship. I saw you all, but I could not call out, for he had tied me up." Mack felt hot blood rise into her face. "He dragged me out of the town and into the hills. I was so, so afraid. Especially in the dark. After a while he did not tie me up. But I knew I had to be good and very careful, or I would be stuck with his knife. He said often enough that he would do so."

"He was a brave boy," Elias proclaimed, and Thomas glowed with pleasure at the praise.

"Then we came upon Mr. Stack that night," Thomas went on. "I dared not speak to him, not knowing then what sort of man he was. All I could think was that I would be sold away to the Natives and never see you again."

Mack pulled him close and kissed his soft cheek. "Nothing like that will ever happen to you now, Thomas," she whispered. "You are safe with me."

"I am most curious, Mr. Stack. How did you learn who Thomas was?" John asked Elias. "How did you make the connection between him and Mack?"

Laughter rumbled in Stack's wide chest. "The little

fiend talks in his sleep," Elias explained, scowling furiously at Thomas in a pretense of disapproval. Thomas just giggled. "I have listened to it every night all the way here. He said Mack's name again and again, very softly that night. Sparks did not hear him, which was Thomas's great good fortune."

Mack set down her goblet of Madeira. "How did you ever convince Sparks to simply turn Thomas over to you?" she asked, not entirely certain she wished to hear the answer.

"I have my ways," Elias assured her, although he did not wish to say more of what he had done from necessity to save the little boy. His voice became very low and solemn. "In the end, the man was not as tough as he talked. You can be certain Mr. Sparks will never harm you or take another child again, Miss Mack. I kept my promise to him, you see."

Mack shut her eyes and drew in a deep breath. Then she slowly it let out and felt herself relax. She could almost hear the words Elias had spoken to Ben Sparks at Molly Ladle's camp. It was over. He was gone. Much later she would think about a life wasted, about all the cruel things done in the name of greed and hatred. For now she felt only an emptiness, as the last of the fear Ben Sparks had caused her drifted away like mist in the sunshine. She opened her eyes and blinked hard to clear them of the rising tears of relief.

The room was very quiet, and then Lieutenant Colonel Smith drummed his fingers on the table in a sharp rap. He gave a small, discreet cough and glanced once at John, whose eyes were fixed on Mack. "Yes, well, good riddance, I say."

"Now, Lieutenant Colonel, sir, my throat is extremely dry from the telling of this tale," Elias boomed.

"My apologies, Mr. Stack. Would you possibly care for more Madeira?" Smith offered.

John stood and stretched luxuriously, ready for bed. "We shall leave the day after tomorrow, sir," he said, yawning behind his hand, and Mack yawned with him, suddenly very tired.

"You shall have supplies from the trade room, ammunition and such. You will use our horses and carts to help carry your gear up past the Falls. And we will arrange for a canoe to be upriver. Back home you will go, Lord MacNeil," Smith pronounced.

Two days later they left Niagara. John carried dispatches for the military at Detroit. It was the least he could do for the kindness Smith and his officers had shown to them. They said their farewells on a damp, drizzly morning and set out. It was not the best day for beginning a voyage, but not one of them would have put it off.

"Take care, Elias," Mack said warmly, and she smiled fondly at the man who had done so much for them. "Give my best regards to Molly Ladle when your paths cross again."

Elias pulled his felt hat from his head and lifted her hand to his lips to kiss it. "Fare thee well, Miss Mack. I shall pass along your greeting." He clasped Jamie's hand in his large paw, and, with a mischievous sideways look at

Mack, said, "Fare thee well, young sir, and although she surely does not need it, do keep your sights fixed on Miss Mack for me until we are all together once more."

And so they parted. Two soldiers were with them to return the cart and horses to the fort once they reached the canoe. John led them on, up the river ten miles or so to the Falls. Standing there, Thomas was stunned into silence. He stared at the Falls in wonder and marveled at the powerful rush of water thundering past. On they went, a few more miles beyond the waterfall, to where their canoe waited on the shore.

Samuel and John pushed the canoe partway into the water. After they loaded their gear and weapons, John picked up Thomas and set him down in the middle.

"You must sit quietly," Mack cautioned the boy. "A canoe is no place to wiggle."

John and Samuel held the canoe against the current. The others climbed in. "There are paddles for all. Jamie in front of Thomas, Mack behind. You there at the bow, Samuel. Hold it steady now." John slid the canoe further into the water, stepped in, and, with a great shove with his paddle, sent them on their way.

Mack picked up the paddle. She had not held one since before they had been kidnapped. How good it was to sit after all the hours of walking. She knew her arms and shoulders would ache with paddling before they stopped for the night, but she did not care. Each stroke would bring them that much closer to Pêche Island.

It was a journey John and Samuel had made many times, and one that Jamie and Mack had taken once before. For Thomas it was all new. When they left the river and set out across Lake Erie, he was certain that it must go on and on and not ever end.

Each night they camped on one beach or another where the sand sloped down to the water. When day returned, they voyaged on along the coast staying close to shore where the waves were smaller. One afternoon when they were halfway down Lake Erie, a storm rose in the distance. Dark clouds tumbled above them and lightning snapped and flashed. Waves began to build, driven by a stiff wind, and the canoe could barely be handled.

"We must stop here," John called to them. "We cannot go on in this! There is a sheltered place just ahead."

Fighting the wind, John turned the canoe and they paddled up a creek far from the roar of the lake. When the storm broke around them, they were ready and sheltered under the canoe. Rain pounded down and drummed on the birchbark. But in less than an hour the clouds moved away, and the setting sun shot the creek with gold.

Mack and the others crawled out. She looked around her. Tall grass waved on the side of the creek. Wildflowers bloomed here and there, and there was a sweet, clean smell. The trees that grew near the shore leaned over, the branches nearly touching the water. Green swallows flew everywhere, swooping and skimming in search of insects. Everything sparkled with the raindrops that the wind shook from the maples and elms.

"What is this place?" Mack asked John. She worked alongside him, preparing their camp for evening, pulling bedrolls out from under the canoe.

"The Ojibwe call it Akiksibi," John told her. He stopped for a moment and ran the back of his sleeve across his sweaty forehead. "I have stayed here many times these years on the way to or from Pêche Island or Fort Niagara. The water is clear, and the hunting and fishing are good. I have often thought that had I not settled on the island, I might have built a cabin here."

"What a perfect spot it is." Mack looked around. "How spectacular the view must be from the cliff up there."

After an evening meal of broiled trout, they climbed the hill and watched the sun sink into Lake Erie. The wind blew hard and whitecaps rolled over the water. Gulls and terns sailed above the lake, riding the updrafts. How lovely this is, Mack thought. She looked out across the lake to the east and south, where she knew the Castle must be. Perhaps someone was watching the sunset from the hills there, just as she was doing here.

Thomas came up beside her and slid his hand into hers. "It does seem as large as the ocean," he declared.

But it was not, and before the week was over, they had reached Lake Erie's west end and approached the mouth of the Detroit River. In the distance a boat was anchored. It pulled hard at the river's current.

"It is the *Swift*!" Jamie called back to John. "I knew her at once!" There was the familiar boat, its mainsail tied neatly on the boom, its single mast of pine gleaming in the sunlight.

John gave a shout and raised his arm in greeting. "That is Wallace and Natka on her. I suspected word would reach them that we were coming home, you see. It is only fitting that they are here to meet us."

Mack felt her heart open when she recognized the boat and the men. "Ahoy, the *Swift*!" she cried.

"Ahoy! Ahoy, the *Swift*!" Jamie echoed. They could hear answering welcomes come across the water.

"Ah, me!" Samuel shouted. "How sad that Natka and Wallace are no wiser than when we were young, John. We nearly wore them out then, and still they come to take us sailing."

The canoe came alongside the boat. The two men leaned down to grab it and passed lines to John and Samuel, who tied the canoe securely. Then they helped Mack and the others onto the deck.

"I heard that!" bellowed Wallace. He stood with his big hands on his hips, his long gray hair pulled back in a club, his worn kilt flapping in the breeze. "I may be an old man, but I dinna think you two could wear me down now any more than you did when you were lads. I only hope that you will not toss up your breakfast, Samuel, as was your habit then." Wallace embraced Samuel and then John. "Welcome home, lads! Welcome home!" He released John, gave Jamie a rough hug, and then kissed Mack heartily on her cheek.

Natka clasped Jamie's hand and then pulled Mack into his arms. Behind him, Wallace beamed at her. They were old men now, the Scot and the Seneca who had watched over John as a boy. In spite of their heavily lined faces, they held themselves straight. Natka pushed her away and held her at arm's length to look her up and down.

"You have changed." He nodded solemnly. The feather he had thrust into his white-streaked scalp lock shivered in the breeze. "You were a girl when you left here. You are a girl no longer." His smile flashed. "It is good to have you back safely, Mack."

"Never fear, Mack!" Samuel shouted. "I will stand between you and the legions of soldiers and warriors at Fort Detroit who will seek your attentions."

"I will sleep well knowing this, Samuel," Mack said over her shoulder. She turned back to Natka. "It is wonderful to be here again."

"And who is this wee lad?" Wallace asked suddenly. For Thomas was standing almost behind Mack, making himself as small as he could.

Jamie made the introductions. "This is Thomas. Wallace, you and he are perfect for each other. You may not know it, but you will surely become the best of friends."

Wallace and Thomas solemnly shook hands. Glancing at Natka, Wallace said "Oh, the things we will show you, lad."

Mack pretended to despair at this. "Thomas, you are fated to become just like John, if they are your tutors."

"Well, they may tutor him later on. For now you are all crew on the *Swift* and should step lively or it will be bread and water tonight!" John commanded in his most nautical tone.

Jamie and Samuel heaved the canoe aboard the *Swift* and tied it down. John took the tiller. Natka pulled up the anchor while Wallace hoisted the mainsail and the jib. Slowly they made their way up the river. There was a good wind at their backs and across the beam for most of the way. The old *Swift* fought against the powerful current to keep moving forward. Now and again she heeled deeply. John would pull the tiller, Wallace would ease a sail, and she would level out.

The boat passed the big islands. Tiny whitecaps danced all around them, and a line of cormorants flew by just above the water. John and the other men talked quietly at the stern. Mack watched them from where she and Jamie sat with Thomas near the bow of the boat. She did not need to hear what John was saying; the expression of deadly anger on Wallace's face and the way Natka squeezed the handle of his tomahawk said it all.

Finally they reached Fort Detroit. The *Swift* slid past the fort's water gate and wooden walls. Mack could see the rooftops of houses just peaking over. A British soldier waved in greeting and yelled something she could not really hear. John waved back.

Then Jamie stood and shouted. "There is it! Look, Thomas! There is Pêche Island."

Mack stood with him. She could see the island in the distance. Just above the sandy beach, its tall, old elms and maples were touched by red in the sunset. Beyond them, sheltered by the woods, John's house and the apple orchard would be waiting. For a while at least, Mack knew she was truly home.

CHAPTER EIGHTEEN

Almost a year passed. It seemed to Mack that those months flowed by as relentlessly as the current of the Detroit River. Summer was for hunting and fishing and tending the kitchen garden planted just beyond the back doorway. Mack spent hours kneeling in the black dirt, pulling weeds from the rows of cabbages, carrots, and sweet herbs. John often went out to sketch alone or with one of the others, for there would always be something new and interesting to draw and send to the Crown. As the King's own artist in Canada, he still felt the old pull of that duty.

Wallace and Natka moved into their summer camp not far from the house, but they came in nearly every evening to join the others for a meal. Samuel remained at the cabin. Thomas would run, or swim, or climb the apple trees in the orchard. Tired of all that, he dug for treasure in a spot where John buried old spoons, broken plate shards, and arrowheads for just that purpose.

That fall they gathered apples, made cider, and did all the things to ready the house and storeroom for the coming winter. Leaves fell in bright showers. When the first flakes of snow drifted onto the island, they had all they needed to pass the winter in comfort.

One day in November, exactly a month before Christmas, they pulled taffy. *La tire*, it was called. It would be saved for the holiday feast. Christmas Eve arrived during a gentle snowfall. Within John's house there was music and singing and enough food to feed everyone at Fort Detroit. Thomas exclaimed over the taffy. A wonderful Yule log of apple wood was lit in the hearth, and at midnight John, Samuel, and Jamie went out to fire their muskets into the dark sky to welcome the coming of Christmas Day. Mack and Thomas watched from the porch, cheering and clapping.

When spring came, Mack and Jamie again went on short trips with John if the weather was good. Mack slept uncomplainingly upon the ground. Strangely, it did not seem so very hard at all, as it had in the wilderness. Life was quiet and peaceful, and for now that was enough.

The wilderness, the Castle. She did not think of them at all, or of Owela either, for that matter. Those things were in the very distant past now. Except for when she saw the corn in the garden, slowly ripening to gold within its cover of green, or when she smelled the tang of wood smoke from a distant campfire as she walked along one of the island's canals on a quiet evening.

Slowly another summer ripened around Mack. In the very early mornings she would walk the beaches of the island in a loosely laced bodice, her petticoat tucked into its waistband, the sleeves of her shift rolled to her elbows. She seldom wore breeches anymore. That sort of clothing she connected with a chapter in her life that had closed as surely as the covers of a book snapped shut. As she walked, the river water felt cool on her ankles and calves. Now and again she found sheepshead stones. One by one she dropped them into her pouch. There they lay, small fingernails of bone that once had led a friend to her.

Letters came from Jane in England.

"Yes, they all say it is madness for you to have stayed, my dear Charlotte," Jane wrote to Mack. "Yet I think it is most amazing that you should know your own heart so well. The Court in London will wait for you, should you ever care to visit it, and I am certain Jamie is correct. You will all be very colorful and completely Canadian the next time we see you here at Brierly."

One morning Mack stood with Thomas on the beach; they were all going out on the *Swift* to fish. Wallace and Natka held the canoe. Just as they were ready to paddle out to where the *Swift* rested at anchor, they saw a group of soldiers who were coming from Fort Detroit in a *bateau*. John waved his arm over his head at the approaching boat. Jamie and Samuel helped the men land their vessel on damp sand.

"It is war, Lord MacNeil," a breathless officer told John. "Word came from Albany by dispatch just yesterday. The rebels in the colonies have risen against the Crown, if you may believe it! There were battles at Lexington and Concord on the nineteenth of April this year 1775. We will not forget that day, I think."

The officer told them more about the furious skirmishes and fighting down in Massachusetts. Lieutenant Colonel Francis Smith had been there leading British troops, but to their great relief, he had not been killed or wounded.

"I knew it would come to this," said John grimly.

"And that so-called patriot, Paul Revere? The man whom we heard assisted Miss MacNeil and your brother?" The officer inclined his head to Mack, but she barely noticed his attentions. "They say he tried to warn the rebels of the British presence, for all the good that did them." Mack turned and walked away, the wind pulling at her skirts. Jamie and Thomas started to follow her, but John called them back.

"Leave her be," he told them. "She needs to be alone at the moment, I believe."

All morning and afternoon Mack walked by herself. Now and again she sat in the sand, her knees drawn to her chest, staring out at the water. How far would the fighting reach? Past the cities of the colonies and into the land that lay there so vulnerable to what might happen? Would the Oneida village withstand a war fought by the revolutionaries and the British? She no longer tried to keep her mind from the Castle and those she knew there.

"Come home, Mack," said a voice behind her. It was John. Thomas and Jamie were there at his side, each holding a candle in a lantern. It was nearly dark. She had not noticed how much time had passed.

Her cape was across Jamie's arm. "Your skirts are

soaked and you will be chilled." His tone was worried. "Here. Put this over your shoulders."

John linked his arm through hers, Jamie held Thomas's hand, and they walked back in silence. When they saw the faint light glowing from the windows of the house, Mack stopped. "Go on ahead, Jamie, Thomas. We will be there in a moment."

Jamie looked from John to Mack. "Come along, Thomas. There is still time for one more wrestling match before we have our dinner."

Mack turned and stared out across the water. Then she faced John. "Are you never lonely? You have no one. Oh, there are your friends, and you have Jamie and me. But do you never feel alone?" She crossed her arms over her chest and held herself tightly. Her voice was small and tired. "I have no idea why I should be, but I am so lonely sometimes, that I can scarcely bear it."

John put his arm around her shoulder and slowly led her back to the house. Oh, Mack, he thought, I will answer you, but it is something you will simply have to learn for yourself or spend your entire life in misery. "Of course, I am lonely at times. Do you think any one of us does not wake in the night and feel alone? But you take what is there. Friendship, family, the kindness of strangers, all those things are like a wall that can hold back loneliness. Besides, I am a great believer in possibility. Who can say what the wind may blow in?" He squeezed her arm. "Come, Mack. I think I smell something delicious for our evening meal."

But Mack had no appetite at dinner and only pushed

the food around on her plate. Later, they sat on the porch at the front of the cabin and watched Thomas trying to catch fireflies.

"I say, John, might we have an outing tomorrow?" Jamie asked suddenly from where he sat on the steps, watching Mack to see what she would say. Reaching down, he pulled out a blade of tender grass and chewed its tip. "More than just a fishing trip, since we did not even do that today."

John leaned back in his chair and put his hands behind his head. "I can see no reason why we might not. The weather is good. It is peaceful here for the time being and there is no threat to our safety."

"What were you thinking of, Jamie?" asked Samuel curiously. "Something exciting, I hope, eh?"

"Can you recall that place on the lake where we stopped as we came back from Niagara?" Jamie asked slowly. He saw that Mack was listening now. "It was when the storm drove us in off the water."

"Akiksibi, it is called," Natka said. "Good fishing there." Wallace nodded in agreement.

"I liked the creek!" Thomas said. He snatched at a firefly. "I remember the sunset on the hill."

"Yes, Akiksibi," John said thoughtfully. "That is the exact spot. Would you sail there, Jamie? I think it is a good idea. You must come along, Samuel, and Thomas needs no coaxing. What do you say to this, Mack?"

They were trying to make her happy. She knew they were aware of her thoughts. How she loved them all. "Yes. It would be pleasant to go out and explore the creek and hills there," she answered in the most cheerful tone she could manage. "We will be gone for some days, I suppose. I will go in and see to our provisions and bedding. Come and help me, Thomas."

Later that evening, they examined the charts in John's study. The journey would take them down the river and halfway down the length of Lake Erie. Wallace and Natka would stay behind, they said, to keep their eyes on the island and house.

"It is too far to sail in one day," John told them. "We might take this route." Jamie and Mack leaned over the chart, watching John slowly trace the way with his finger. "Down the river and onto the lake. We could anchor out at Pelee, this big island here, and then sail on the next day. Or we can sail all night. There is something wonderful about being aboard a sailboat on the lake at night."

"Yes," Mack decided for them. "That is what we will do. A night sail would be perfect."

The next morning a west wind blew. At dawn they paddled out to where the *Swift* was anchored in the cove. When all that they needed was loaded and stowed, they pulled the canoe on board and tied it securely. John raised the sails and let them flap. With Mack at the tiller, Samuel and Jamie pulled up the anchor. Thomas ran about wildly until Mack threatened to tie him to the mast. Then quickly John hoisted the sails.

Mack felt her spirits lighten as the wind filled the canvas and they moved out of the cove and onto the river. The breeze was steady and strong, and, carried by the river's current, they flew along the water. The sailboat passed Fort Detroit and each of the islands that lay in the river, scattering feeding gulls and ducks. All morning they sailed, taking turns at the tiller under John's watchful eyes, until Lake Erie lay before them at the river's mouth.

"We will change course and head eastward down the coastline," called John. They hauled in the sails. Mack, who was again at the tiller, pulled it hard, and the *Swift* turned her bow toward Akiksibi.

All the rest of that day they journeyed along Lake Erie, taking turns at the helm. In the evening, the sun dropped into the water behind them and the moon rose. Stars appeared in the clear night sky. Mack tucked Thomas in to sleep in *Swift*'s small, low cabin. She felt tired and content.

All night the *Swift* sailed down the lake through the darkness. A full moon turned the water to silver, and the sun that rose the next morning rippled it with red. When they reached the mouth of the creek at Akiksibi that afternoon, Mack was sunburned and almost happy. They dropped the sails and anchored some distance up the creek as they had nearly a year ago.

"Let us stay right here." Mack smiled, looking around her. "It is a good place to camp, so untouched and empty of people." It was as lovely as she remembered. Ducks swam in the green water. Now and again a fish jumped. Large trees leaned over the creek and covered the hills on each side of the water.

"Good enough," said Jamie. What a relief to see her

smiling once more.

Later, they watched the sun slowly begin to set while they relaxed around the low fire. It would be a clear day tomorrow, and they should catch many fish here, someone said lazily. Mack sat with her feet in the creek's water, wiggling her bare toes. Only Thomas did not seem at all tired. He raced up and down the banks of the creek, hitting a leather ball with a lacrosse stick. Thomas gave the ball a hard slap, and it flew into the bushes. For a moment he disappeared into the brush after it. Then, with the ball in his hand, Thomas came out at a dead run.

"You had best get up and come with me, John," Thomas announced seriously. He looked over his shoulder and back again to where John lay stretched out on the grass.

John looked up from his comfortable position. "Do I look like a complete fool, my lad?" John asked. "I will not be ambushed by a wild youngster with a lacrosse stick, his mind set on mischief."

"There is someone coming," Thomas insisted, and then a brilliant idea occurred to him. "I will drive him away and into the lake with balls of mud from the creek, if you wish. They fly very far when you fling them with a lacrosse stick!"

John looked over at the others, and, without a word, they found their muskets and stood together. Mack got to her feet, as well, untangling herself from her skirts. At first, she could not see who was walking toward them through the trees and bushes. John and Jamie called out happy greetings, and then the stranger lifted his head and looked across the clearing to where Mack waited. It was no stranger at all.

Owela had journeyed for some weeks to find the island that lay in a swiftly flowing river. He had been told the route — he was still at least five days' journeying from his destination — but he was in no rush. He had traveled slowly so that he might think and carefully plan what he hoped he was brave enough to say. For some days he had camped here on the lake's shore, his canoe pulled up on the sand and hidden by brush.

In the late afternoon he had watched as the boat sailed up the creek. Happiness filled him when he saw who was on it. But he needed time to prepare himself carefully.

He had built a small sweat lodge from fresh cedar bows that morning. The stones heated, steam rising around him, he sat inside it. There he cleansed his mind and let his heart open. Then, rubbing his body briskly with cold water from the lake, he had dressed carefully in the clothing he had carried all the way from the Oneida Castle. He wore a shirt of white linen and leggings of deep blue blanket cloth, beaded down their length and edged with red satin ribbon. His hair hung loose upon his shoulders, and the silver locket rested outside the shirt on his chest. He held his musket with one hand; a bundle was slung over his shoulder.

"Well, Owela, you have come all this distance just to see us this fine evening," Jamie said as he leaned upon his musket. "You have missed me so very much?"

Owela's eyes crinkled as he smiled. "*Sheko:li*, Jamie,"

he said. "It is most pleasant to see you as well." Then he took a deep breath and turned his eyes back to Mack, who waited in watchful silence. "*Sheko:li*, Mack."

"*Sheko:li*, Owela," she answered softly. "You have come a very long way, my friend."

"Indeed, friend," he admitted. "It was a long way, but there was something I thought that I might tell you, and since you were on John's island, nothing would do except that I make the voyage. How odd to find you here!"

"Not so odd, perhaps," Mack answered with a small laugh. "I have long since stopped wondering why things happen the way they do."

"I, too," Owela replied. "If I was to tell you this thing, though, first I must ask your kin for permission to do so." John inclined his head just a little. "And then I would make a gift to the men of your clan. Just to let them know that I am a capable hunter."

Owela shifted the bundle and set it on the ground near Jamie and John. Fox and muskrat pelts and the fine furs of marten and beaver shone in the sunshine. Jamie dropped to his knees and ran his hands over the pelts, while John nodded in approval at this generosity and skill.

Owela cleared his throat and took a deep breath. "I have thought for some time that I might look for a home of my own," he went on, looking off into the distance. "Not so far from the Castle that I might not visit there, and yet a new place, perhaps."

"Just where might that place be?" Mack asked carefully.

"Well, now, I thought it must be near water. There are many lakes and rivers to choose from, but it might even be a place like this one. I would build a longhouse at first and then a cabin of logs. Not small, so a person felt closed in, but a roomy home with windows with glass panes that might be opened to let in the sunshine and the clean air. There would be a boat, as well. A canoe to begin with, and later a small sailing boat, I think. And someone to share it all with."

"It does sound wonderful," said Mack quietly. "That would be a happy life, I believe."

"Indeed, if that person was willing to work to make that life," Owela went on, "for there would be a great deal of hard work. It must be someone who knows the land the way I do, someone who would want a houseful of young ones." Mack blushed a bit at this to her annoyance, but Owela did not seem to notice.

"Children do make a house come to life," Mack told him, looking over at Thomas.

"It would be a big family, and a life that stretched from the Castle to our home and to wherever that person's kin dwelled. It need not be all one way or the other. To meet someone halfway is best. For there is no reason, I have come to think, that people cannot live at least a little in both worlds."

"Yes, you are correct," Mack agreed firmly. "Both worlds and one that they make for themselves." Owela nodded and smiled at her. She understood.

"I like this story. Is it a true one?" asked Thomas, his wide eyes fastened on Owela.

"It could be, Thomas," Owela answered. Then he turned back to Mack and said in a low voice, "If I told you all that, Mack, what might you say?"

No one spoke as they all watched her and waited.

"I would say yes, Owela," she answered him simply.

"Let us go up the hill," Owela's voice broke a little with happiness. "The sun will just be going down into the lake, and that would be a fine thing to see."

Thomas jumped up and led the way. There was a great deal of teasing and laughter and talking as they all started up the hill. Mack and Owela followed a little behind the others, her warm hand held tightly in his.

When all was quiet and the sound of their footsteps rustling in the bushes died away, a large dragonfly darted from the rushes at the edge of the creek. It had not been above the water for very long. The warm weather had called to it to come up from the creek's mud where it had lived until today. It hovered for a moment, keen, faceted eyes taking in the world, and then in a flash of red and blue it sailed into the sky to see what it might find. For like the young and hopeful couple who climbed the hill, its adventure had begun.

AUTHOR'S NOTE

By the Standing Stone is a work of fiction based upon events in the eighteenth century. Most of the characters in the book are imaginary. Two, however, did play important roles in the Revolutionary War. Paul Revere was the patriot this story paints him. On a number of occasions he and his horse carried word to the revolutionaries of danger from British forces.

Lieutenant Colonel Francis Smith also lived during that period. He left Fort Niagara for Quebec in the summer of 1774. Later he commanded a British column that marched against the rebels at two small villages called Lexington and Concord. History has referred to that first musket fired as "the shot heard round the world," so far-reaching was its effect. Both Revere and Smith were there at Lexington, and so would have heard it.

It was not simply the British military and the Americans who fought. Each side had its Native allies. The Oneida and Tuscarora peoples became the allies of the revolutionaries, while the rest of the Six Nations Confederacy sided with the British. Many remarkable stories of their bravery and steadfastness are documented.

But the price was high. In 1779, George Washington, commander of the revolutionary army, moved against the Loyalists and the Natives who fought with the British. Homes, villages, and crops were destroyed all through central New York. The Natives fled to Fort Niagara, and, eventually, thousands were living all around the fort with little to sustain them. Those within Fort Niagara spent a grim winter. There was a shortage of food, blankets, and medicine. But the Natives outside the fort suffered horribly and that winter hundreds either died of starvation or froze to death from exposure. Native storytellers call it "The Winter of Hunger."

The Oneidas lost their villages and land, the Oneida Castle was destroyed, and at least a third of their people died. Sadly, the fact that Native people stood by their allies created a civil war amongst the tribes, one that was long in healing, but the Six Nations stand well and whole today.

By the Standing Stone is in some ways a personal story, since there is a third character in the work who did live at Fort Detroit at one time. Marie, the ghostly presence whom John MacNeil can never forget, was my grandmother many generations back. She was the daughter of Pierre Roy and Marguerite Ouabankikove, a Miami woman. Marie married Pierre LaButte. She died of smallpox, leaving behind one son; and it is through Marie and her son that I trace my Métis blood.

As for Akiksibi, it is a very real place, all old trees and

windswept cliffs that loom over Lake Erie. I have often stood there myself and looked out across the water, for high on that cliff is where I make my home at Brierly in Port Stanley today. What tales of adventure the lake and shores would tell if only they could speak. But since they cannot, I try to tell the stories for them.

ACKNOWLEDGEMENTS

A ship does not sail itself. It takes people to do that. Like a grand frigate that cannot exist without its sailors, a loyal and helpful crew played an important role in the creation of *By the Standing Stone*. My husband and captain, William, with whom I sail on our own vessel, *Windseeker I*, provided a safe haven on the stormy seas of writing. My great appreciation goes to my publisher, Kathryn Cole, who helped me look closely at what was most important. Lynne Missen, my editor, again worked her magic in fine-tuning the manuscript, and Al Van Mil created a wonderful image for the cover of the book. My thanks to them both.

Ellis Delahoy read the manuscript with Fort Niagara and the outlying regions in mind. His knowledge of the fort and its history was invaluable. He is a seasoned re-enactor connected with Schuyler's Company, New York Provincials. The original company fought in the French and Indian Wars. I owe him a further debt of gratitude for kindly permitting me to use the name and character of Elias Stack. Mr. Stack is Ellis' persona in

Living History, and they are both fine gentlemen, indeed.

To Larry Lozon for supplying the image of the pistol that appears upon the book's cover, and to Tim Shaw for information regarding the sad time at Fort Niagara referred to by Native storytellers as "The Winter of Hunger," my thanks. Pat Cornelius and Joan Doxtator, Oneida women with whom I work, were very helpful regarding Oneida language and customs. My thanks for sharing your culture with me.

My appreciation goes out to Andy Gallup, historian and writer, who read the manuscript and made many suggestions regarding eighteenth-century details. He continues to be a source of inspiration in both this century and the eighteenth century. Like me, Andy is a member of *Le Detachement*, a remarkable *compagnie* of people who interpret the history of New France. We attempt to make history come alive. For if the past lives — especially through books — then those who made the sacrifices, fought the battles, and gave us those stories will live once more.